Ethan stoo
house to w
return.

Sara opened the door. Her lips curved in a shy smile. She stepped aside, and he had to force his feet over the threshold.

"Well, what do you think?"

Ethan slowly scanned the sparkling clean room. "I, uh, it's fine, Sara. The place looks real nice." Clearing his throat, he moved back a step. "I think I'll just go—"

"You're leaving?"

The disappointment in her voice sent a flush of pleasure through him. "Actually, I was just going to get something from my truck."

She smiled.

Ethan headed out the door, calling himself every kind of a dumb jerk. He didn't even like petite, fair-haired women. So why was he getting all tongue-tied and weak-kneed?

He was getting worked up over nothing. Of course he would have a reaction to a woman. He hadn't had female company in a mighty long time. By his own choice, he reminded himself. And he wanted to keep it that way.

But he couldn't, if Sara kept smiling at him.

Dear Reader,

Happy New Year! May this year bring you happiness, good health and all that you wish for. And at Harlequin American Romance, we're hoping to provide you with a year full of heartwarming books that you won't be able to resist.

Leading the month is *The Secretary Gets Her Man* by Mindy Neff, Harlequin American Romance's spin-off to Harlequin Intrigue's TEXAS CONFIDENTIAL continuity series. This exciting story focuses on the covert operation's much-mentioned wallflower secretary, Penny Archer.

Muriel Jensen's *Father Formula* continues her successful WHO'S THE DADDY? series about three identical sisters who cause three handsome bachelors no end of trouble when they discover one woman is about to become a mother. Next, after opening an heirloom hope chest, a bride-to-be suddenly cancels her wedding and starts having intimate dreams about a handsome stranger, in *Have Gown, Need Groom.* This is the first book of Rita Herron's new miniseries THE HARTWELL HOPE CHESTS. And Debbi Rawlins tells the emotional story of a reclusive rancher who opens his home—and his heart— to a lovely single mother, in *Loving a Lonesome Cowboy.*

In February, look for another installment in the RETURN TO TYLER series with *Prescription for Seduction* by Darlene Scalera.

Wishing you happy reading,

Melissa Jeglinski
Associate Senior Editor
Harlequin American Romance

LOVING A
LONESOME COWBOY
Debbi Rawlins

TORONTO • NEW YORK • LONDON
AMSTERDAM • PARIS • SYDNEY • HAMBURG
STOCKHOLM • ATHENS • TOKYO • MILAN • MADRID
PRAGUE • WARSAW • BUDAPEST • AUCKLAND

ISBN 0-373-16860-8

LOVING A LONESOME COWBOY

Visit us at www.eHarlequin.com

Printed in U.S.A.

ABOUT THE AUTHOR

Debbi Rawlins currently lives with her husband and dog in Las Vegas, Nevada. A native of Hawaii, she married on Maui and has since lived in Cincinnati, Chicago, Tulsa, Houston, Detroit and Durham, NC, during the past twenty years. Now that she's had enough of the gypsy life, it'll take a crane, a bulldozer and a forklift to get her out of her new home. Good thing she doesn't like to gamble. Except maybe on romance.

Books by Debbi Rawlins

HARLEQUIN AMERICAN ROMANCE

HARLEQUIN INTRIGUE

SINGLE MOTHER SEEKS...

Job as a housekeeper. I will clean your house till it shines and cook meals guaranteed to make you sigh. If you have children, I can even charm them into behaving for you. (At least, I'll try!)

Please call Sara Conroy, at 555-2725.

And if you happen to be a brooding-but-oh-so-handsome cowboy, I might just find my way into your heart....

Chapter One

Ethan Slade parked his old pickup in front of Manny's General Store, ignoring the stares and whispers of the midday crowd as he climbed out and headed for the post office. Most folks wouldn't expect to see him in town so close to Christmas, and they all had to be wondering what he was doing here. But other than a nod or a brief greeting, no one said a word. They wouldn't. Not when he employed most of their brothers, sons and fathers.

The responsibility of owning the second-largest ranch in Central New Mexico, which made him the town's major employer, was one of two reasons that kept him here.

The other was Emily's grave.

Simon Whitefeather looked up from the mail he was sorting and his black eyes immediately narrowed over his wire-rimmed reading glasses. "Mornin', Ethan, what brings you into town? Weren't you here just five months ago?"

Ethan slowly nodded. "I'm out of supplies. Any mail for me in the back?"

"Nope. Sam picked up the ranch mail two days

ago, bills and catalogues mostly.'' Simon frowned and scratched his balding head. "Seems to me Billy Bob has a telegram for you. Unless he already got it to you?" When Ethan shook his head, Simon added, "It came about two or three days ago. He said he was going to run it out to the ranch."

Ethan rubbed the back of his neck. Who the hell would be sending him a telegram? Jenna. It had to be his kid sister. He wondered what kind of scrape she'd gotten into now. It seemed that was the only time he heard from her anymore.

"I told him he'd have to leave it with Sam. I figured you're still living out at the caretaker's shack."

"Thanks, Simon." Ethan had known the older man a long time. They'd met near Miller's Creek when Ethan and Sam were only six. Simon had taught them how to swim. Ethan knew Simon would respect his desire not to have Billy Bob Simms or anyone else nosing anywhere near the shack.

"Can't swear he'll listen. I heard he's bucking for a job at the Double S."

"Things are slow this time of year. I doubt Sam needs an extra hand." Even though Ethan owned the place, he rarely interfered with the way Sam ran things. He preferred mending fences, herding strays, preserving his solitude. "How's Martha doing?"

"Complaining about her arthritis in one breath, and that I don't take her anywhere in the other. Women. If I live to be a hundred, I'll never understand 'em."

"Yeah, I know what you mean." Ethan stooped to pick up a plastic snowman that had fallen off the counter. He stuck it next to the Santa sitting in the middle of the cotton snow, then headed toward the door. "Tell her I said to take care of herself."

"Ethan?"

Reluctantly he stopped at the door, wishing like hell he hadn't come to town today. Thirty years of friendship made him turn around. "Yeah?"

"Martha keeps asking when you're coming to dinner."

He exhaled slowly. "I've been pretty busy lately...."

"You gotta be taking Christmas off. She roasts a mean goose."

"I don't think—"

"She serves it with her homemade cranberry sauce. That took the County Fair blue ribbon three years in a row."

Ethan half smiled. "I'll think about it."

"You do that." Their gazes met, understanding and sympathy in Simon's eyes. Ethan had to look away. "There won't be anyone there but us, and of course, Sam's invited, too."

"Thanks, Simon, I'll let you know." Ethan opened the door and stepped outside, grateful for the brisk winter air.

He inhaled a lungful, then turned up the collar of his jacket in deference to the chill nipping at his neck. No way would he go to the Whitefeathers' house for Christmas. Holidays were still too painful. Emily should have been here sharing them with him, having his children, growing old with him. Not buried under six feet of cold ground.

He swallowed and adjusted his Stetson before

heading toward Manny's store. After Ethan picked
up several month's supply of canned goods and toi-
letries, he'd have to go find out about that telegram.
He doubted Sam had it. If he did, he would have
run it over to Ethan right away. Sam was a lot more
than his foreman, he was the best friend a man could
have.

Just outside Manny's, Billy Bob hollered Ethan's
name, then ran across the street, nearly getting run
over by a white Jeep Wrangler.

He waved an envelope. "I saw your truck. Figured I'd catch up with you sooner or later. I got a
telegram here for you from Jenny." He handed it to
Ethan, then dragged his sleeve across his red, runny
nose. "What is it she's calling herself these days?"

"Jenna." Ethan started to tear open the telegram,
then frowned at Billy Bob, whose gaze was glued
to the envelope. Ethan dug into his pocket, came up
with a five-dollar bill and put it in Billy's hand.
"Thanks, kid."

"Gee, thank *you,* Mr. Slade." He waited for
Ethan to open it.

"Don't you have something else to do?"

The young man's eyes lifted to Ethan's expres-
sionless face and widened slightly. "Yeah, sure."
Billy Bob took a step back and shrugged. "If you
wanna answer it, I guess you'll let me know."

"I reckon I will." He didn't go back to tearing
the envelope until Billy turned to leave.

"Oh, Mr. Slade?"

Ethan looked up.

"They just opened one of those big supermarkets
over in Andersonville," Billy said, with a small

sheepish smile. "My mom tells me they have a real nice floral section year round. You know, for... when..."

Ethan stiffened slightly. "I appreciate you letting me know."

"No problem." The young man met Ethan's eyes for a moment, then he shoved his hands in his pockets and shuffled away.

"Hey, Billy."

He turned. "Yeah?"

"If you're needing a part-time job, go see Sam. Tell him I sent you."

"Gee, thanks, Mr. Slade."

Ethan nodded, then headed down the opposite end of the sidewalk while he fished the telegram out of the envelope. He stopped suddenly and stared at his sister's message in stunned disbelief.

Even the rousing chorus of *Deck the Halls* coming from Manny's store couldn't drown out Ethan's involuntary curse.

SARA CONROY zipped the front of her daughter's jacket, then adjusted Misty's thick wool scarf to make sure her neck was covered.

"It's not cold enough to wear all this stuff, Mom." Misty scowled as she tried to loosen the scarf.

"It will be once we get outside." Silently, Sara agreed. The weather wasn't cold enough yet to warrant wool, but she'd expected milder New Mexico to have colder weather. Besides, she'd brought precious few clothes, only what she'd been able to sneak out of the house, and the scarf would have to do.

"Can't I just put it on later if I need it?"

Sara looked into her five-year-old's pleading blue eyes and relented. A little nippy air wasn't going to harm Misty. Especially not after what Sara had put the child through in the past month. "Okay, but if I say it's too cold, you put it on immediately with no argument."

Misty grinned and yanked off the scarf.

When she tossed it on the bed, Sara gathered it up before letting them out of the small motel room and making sure the rickety lock had engaged behind them. The motel she'd chosen was rundown and shabby, but it seemed safe enough, especially in a small town like Sedina. Anyway, it wasn't fear of strangers that kept her looking over her shoulder, or double-checking locks.

She took Misty's hand as they walked the short distance to town, hoping that the apple and cheese and crackers she'd given her daughter for lunch would stay with her until they returned. Until Sara got a job and padded their meager nest egg, there'd be no more restaurant meals for them.

After two attempts to get Misty to talk, they ended up making the five-minute walk in silence. Although her daughter had always been a shy quiet child, Sara had noticed an increased withdrawal since they'd left Dallas, and she tried not to push.

It was difficult, though, because even while she knew they'd done the right thing by leaving, she felt horrible guilt. Especially when Misty's eyes lit up when they passed store windows, displaying all the latest toys for Christmas. There was no way Sara would be able to afford the kind of lavish Christmas Misty was used to, and if no one answered Sara's ad soon, they could very well be spending Christmas morning in the train station.

Shivering at the thought, she hurried them toward Della's House of Beauty and one of two bulletin boards where she'd placed her ad. She stared in dismay. Below the neatly printed offer of holiday housecleaning, she'd included a row of easy-to-tear-off strips with the motel's phone number. Not a single one had been taken.

She swallowed hard, then forced a smile for Misty. "Okay, let's walk over to Manny's store."

"Can I have an ice-cream sundae?"

"It's too cold for ice cream, honey." And ice cream was too expensive. But at Misty's disappointed expression, Sara added, "How about a cherry sucker?"

Her daughter lifted a shoulder. "I guess."

"Come on." She ruffled Misty's strawberry-blond curls, then tugged her down the sidewalk. "That's your favorite."

Manny's was crowded today, and several people stood near the door talking and blocking Sara's view of the bulletin board. When she finally ducked in close enough to see, her heart fell. Again, no one had taken a single phone number.

She shouldn't be disappointed or surprised, she told herself. In a town this small and remote, people probably didn't hire domestic help. Sara herself hadn't grown up with that kind of luxury. It wasn't until she'd married Cal that she'd had a maid to

make her bed each morning and a cook to provide
their meals.

Now, she'd give anything for the opportunity to
scrub someone else's floor. It would mean a Christmas tree and presents for Misty.

"Come on, kiddo, let's go get that sucker I promised you." She gave her daughter a bright smile,
then froze when she saw a man stop at the bulletin
board and finger her ad.

He was tall, slim, his hair dark and kind of long,
what she could see of it under his black Stetson. The
blue denim jacket he wore was faded nearly gray,
his jeans were well-worn and so were his boots.

After staring at the ad for a moment, he withdrew
a piece of paper from an envelope, read it, then
looked at the ad again. Although his posture was
straight and proud, there was a slight slump to his
shoulders that gave him an air of defeat. When he
reached out and tore off one of the strips with her
phone number, her heart thudded.

"I thought we were going to buy my sucker."

Sara glanced at her daughter, then tugged her
closer, her gaze shooting back to the man. "We will,
honey, in just a minute."

When he turned around, Sara bowed her head
slightly and averted her eyes. It wouldn't do to have
a prospective employer see her spying on him. She
waited until he started to pass them and briefly gave
him a sideways glance.

She was only quick enough to catch his profile
and the fact that he was badly in need of a shave.
What ultimately drew her attention was the wide

berth others seemed to give him and the stares and whispers in his wake.

Great. She finally had a hot prospect and he was probably the town ax murderer. She sighed. She sure knew how to attract the misfits, just like honey drew flies.

She watched him walk away, surprised at the slight stirring in her chest when he stopped and one side of his mouth lifted at two little girls. He tipped his Stetson to them and they giggled, then ran off.

Just then Judy Hawkins, who owned the corner diner, came out of Manny's. Sara had gotten to know her a little when she and Misty had first come to town and they could afford to eat there twice a day.

"Hi, Sara, Misty." Judy shifted her grocery bag to her other arm. "I haven't seen you two this past week."

"I've been dieting." Sara shrugged, too embarrassed to admit the truth. She was almost broke.

Judy let out a howl of laughter. "Lose another ounce and you'll be wearing Misty's clothes."

Misty made a face. "We didn't bring that much."

Sara squeezed her daughter's hand. Now wasn't the time for her suddenly to get talkative. "See that man over there?" Sara nodded toward the guy who'd seemed interested in her ad, already turning the corner. "Do you know who he is?"

Judy craned her neck and frowned. "The one who just disappeared down Second Street? Looked like Ethan Slade, except he doesn't come to town much any more." Judy stared curiously at Sara. "Did he have dark hair, brown eyes and a deep cleft in his chin?'' Sara nodded. ''That's Ethan, all right, nice piece of man flesh, but you don't want to get mixed up with him.''

Heat climbed Sara's face at the implication in the older woman's tone. She should set the record straight, tell Judy why she'd asked about him, but pride held Sara back. ''It's not what you think—''

A horn blasted, and Judy's gaze shot toward the street. ''There's my ride. See you at the diner, huh?''

Sara nodded and watched her hurry toward the dirty white sedan. Since she only knew Judy casually, it was difficult to read her expression, but in spite of her warning, Judy hadn't seemed afraid of or horrified by the man. There had almost been a trace of sympathy in her eyes.

Sara's gaze strayed toward the corner of Second and Main. Still, Judy had said not to get mixed up with him, and the last thing Sara needed was any more trouble. As much as she hated to, instinct told her she'd better let this opportunity slide....

''Come on, Mom.'' Misty tugged at her hand, and Sara snapped out of her trance.

''Okay, we'll go get your sucker, and let's pick up another jar of peanut butter.''

Misty made a face.

Sara brushed the bangs out of her eyes. ''I thought that was your favorite?''

''Not every day.''

Sara flinched. ''I know, sweetie. We'll look for something else, too, okay?''

They passed a newspaper stand on the way into the store and Sara made a mental note to pick up a paper even though she already knew there weren't many jobs available that would allow her to keep Misty with her. But it didn't look like her ad was paying off, and she would have to do something soon.

In the corner, just past the two clerks busily ringing up sales, a man collected toys for the needy. His box overflowed with brightly wrapped presents and some dolls and trucks that weren't wrapped.

"Oh, Mommy." Misty's eyes widened, and she tugged on Sara's hand. "Can I have that doll with the long red braid?"

Sara smiled down at her. "Sorry, honey, but those things are for the poor and homeless."

Misty looked up, her big blue eyes full of innocence. "But that's us, isn't it, Mommy?"

Sara blinked, her head suddenly growing so light that she thought she might pass out. Swallowing around the lump in her throat, she bent down and gave Misty a hug. "Come on, baby, we have to hurry back to the motel."

She hoped she hadn't already missed Ethan Slade's call.

HAVING TO GO to town two days in a row had Ethan in a foul mood. All because of Jenna. He couldn't wait to get his hands on his sister. He didn't care that he hadn't seen her in six years, he was going to wring her neck anyway.

He steered the truck into the motel parking lot and squinted at the numbers on the orange doors, looking for the room number Sara Conroy had given him over the phone. There was an empty parking stall in front of number six and as soon as he pulled in and turned off the engine, the door opened. A petite woman with reddish-blond hair stepped outside, and quietly closed the door behind her.

She gave him a shy smile, then rubbed her palms down the front of her jeans while she waited for him to walk around the front of the pickup.

"Mr. Slade?"

He nodded. "Ethan."

"I'm Sara Conroy," she said, offering him her hand.

It trembled slightly in his grasp, and although her blue eyes met his steadily, wariness darkened them.

"You're awfully young."

She blinked and pulled back her hand. "That has nothing to do with how well I can clean. Besides, I'm not that young."

Ethan rubbed the side of his jaw. He supposed that was true, except he didn't know that some pretty young gal would want to do the dirty job that he had in mind. Besides, she was little, and there was going to be some lifting involved in restoring the house.

Still, he figured he was lucky to find someone at this late date, and that she was a stranger and not likely to pry was a big bonus.

"This is going to be a sizable job. The house hasn't been lived in for almost six years," he finally said. "It'll probably take you the two full days."

"No problem."

"Like I told you on the phone, the girls get here on Friday, which basically gives you no leeway."

Shrugging, she pushed back the sleeves of her

pink flannel shirt. She had the tiniest wrists he'd ever seen. "Like I told you, no problem."

He leaned against the front of his truck. She hadn't asked him inside, and he didn't blame her. He was a stranger to her. Made him wonder what she'd found out about him. A cautious woman would have asked around. "I won't be around to help."

"I won't need it."

Ethan exhaled. "You have a car?"

She shook her head.

"The ranch is about thirty miles outside of town. How do you plan on getting there?"

She smiled. "I can be ready in twenty minutes."

He stiffened. It wasn't like it was out of his way, but he'd planned on asking Sam to let her in. Although he probably ought to make sure she only readied the kitchen and the rooms his nieces would need. No sense in putting the entire house back to order. But it had been a hell of a long time since he'd set foot in that house. And he wasn't sure if he was ready. He liked living alone in the caretaker's shack. Life was fine just the way it was.

He lifted his Stetson off his head, pushed the too-long strands of hair off his forehead, then settled the hat back down. "All right. I was going to let the foreman take care of things, but I suppose I can let you in and make sure you know where everything is."

Her smile broadened. "Great." Dusting her hands together, she turned to the door, then stopped. "Maybe you have something to do in town while I get ready? I won't be but twenty minutes."

He looked at his watch. The worn leather band was on its last leg. Maybe he ought to use the time to replace it. ''Twenty minutes,'' he said, and rounded the truck to the door.

By the time he'd climbed behind the wheel, Sara had already disappeared behind the ugly orange door. He couldn't help but wonder why a pretty young girl like her was staying in a dumpy motel like this. Or why she needed a job cleaning other people's houses.

Maybe she was a runaway. Just like his sister had been once upon a time. Sara had to be younger than Jenna. He turned the key in the ignition, his thoughts straying to his sister.

In some ways it seemed like only yesterday that he'd awakened at sunup to find a note from Jenna telling him she'd eloped. But she'd been seventeen then, and now she was sending her two daughters to spend Christmas with him while she honeymooned with her soon-to-be-third husband.

Ethan sighed heavily. What the hell was he going to do with a twelve- and six-year-old for ten days? It wasn't that he didn't like children, or that he wasn't happy to see his nieces, but he obviously didn't know beans about kids.

He'd tried his hardest to raise fourteen-year-old Jenna after their parents had died, but he'd clearly failed. She'd gone from a sweet-tempered, shy child to a headstrong hellion by the time she was sixteen. Of course he'd only been twenty himself at the time of the car accident, and totally clueless about the needs of a young teenage girl. The only thing he knew about was ranching. And Emily.

But Emily was dead now. And Ethan didn't give a damn anymore about the ranch they'd built together. Sam took care of everything just fine.

There was a small jewelry and coin store right at the edge of town, so he parked the truck and went inside. He vaguely knew the owner, who was reading a comic book behind the counter, but fortunately not well enough to make small talk or to have to answer a lot of nosy questions. Other than that, no one else was around. Probably all home having supper.

The owner showed him a modest selection of watchbands from which to choose, then went back to reading his comic book. Ethan checked the time. He still had ten minutes.

He tried to concentrate on finding the most durable band, but his mind kept drifting to the girls' arrival. Erika was the older one; he'd seen her only twice before, on the rare occasions when Jenna had remembered she still had family and had shown up at the ranch. Denise, the younger one, had to be about six. He'd never met her or her father.

His gut clenched at the thought that these two little girls were his own flesh and blood—the last of the Slade line. He and Emily had waited on having children. Foolishly, they'd counted on having a lifetime together.

He quickly chose a plain black leather band before his thoughts wandered to forbidden territory, then he pulled some money out of his pocket while the owner replaced the old band. Already twenty minutes had flown by, and damn if it wasn't going to take Sara Conroy every spare minute to get the house in decent shape.

As he left the store, his thoughts strayed back to her. He sure hoped she was stronger than she looked. He wouldn't be much help to her. The idea of going back to the house still made him uneasy. The idea of even Sara or his nieces entering the house and touching things didn't sit well with him.

He forced a deep breath as he fished in his pocket for his keys. In a way, it was better Jenna had given him no notice. He didn't have time to dread facing the ghosts or the memories.

Besides, he had enough to worry about, trying to figure out what to do with two kids.

He opened the truck's door and froze.

Sara was already sitting in the cab. On her lap was a suitcase. Beside her was a freckled-faced little girl staring back at him.

Chapter Two

"Who is this?"

Sara raised her brows in innocence, then looked down at the child who had plastered herself to Sara's side. "You mean, Misty? She's my daughter. Misty, say hi to Mr. Slade."

Misty didn't utter so much as a peep.

"Why is she sitting in my truck?"

Sara set a pair of headphones over Misty's ears, then started the Baby Beluga tape she'd readied in the event Mr. Slade opposed her plan. "You didn't expect me to leave her alone in the motel room, did you?"

"I didn't expect her at all." Ethan frowned at the suitcase. "What's that for?"

"I wasn't sure I'd get a ride back so I brought a few things in case we have to spend the night." In fact, Sara was counting on it. She'd already checked out of the motel, hoping to save a couple of nights' rent.

"You're not spending the night."

"But it makes sense."

"Not to me."

"Don't you think you should get in? Standing on the sidewalk isn't going to solve anything."

Ethan climbed behind the wheel, his expression grim as he stared straight ahead. "You don't understand."

"Is it the owner? Do you think he'd have a problem with me staying in his house?"

"Possibly."

Sara rubbed her left temple. She hadn't considered that problem. But, of course, she was a stranger to this man, and whoever owned the house. "You said the owner doesn't live there anymore, right?"

He nodded, slowly turning to look at her.

She gave him a bright smile. "Then surely there isn't anything of value left in the house."

His head jerked a little, almost as though she'd struck out at him.

"I only meant that he wouldn't have to worry about me stealing anything." Heat climbed her face, and she automatically slipped an arm around Misty. "Not that I'm a thief. But I am a stranger to you."

He shook his head, and brought his troubled gaze to hers. "The thought never crossed my mind. What about you? Aren't you concerned about me?"

She stared back at him, wondering what had made his eyes so sad. They were a warm shade of brown, a sort of milk chocolate color, but they lacked sparkle or expression. "I asked around about you."

He seemed to tense, then looked straight ahead again.

That made her all the more curious. Neither of the two people besides Judy that she'd asked had had an unkind thing to say about Ethan Slade. In fact, they wouldn't say much at all. Only that he was an honorable man, and she needn't worry. She'd shoved her curiosity aside and asked no more questions. She wouldn't ask him any either. She of all people knew the importance of privacy. Of keeping secrets.

"Shouldn't we get moving before it gets too late?" she prompted, hoping he hadn't changed his mind.

He stared in silence for another minute, and when he finally turned the key and started the engine, her breath slipped out in relief.

"Certain rooms will be off limits to both you and your daughter," he said, without looking at her. "I'll point them out as soon as we get there. About food for tonight and tomorrow morning...," he slid her a look, and she was surprised to see concern in his eyes. "There may be a few canned goods, but nothing else. I can't even be sure the refrigerator is still working."

"No problem. We still have a jar of peanut butter and crackers and a couple of bananas. We'll be fine."

His concern gave way to curiosity, but he said nothing as he returned his attention to the road.

Sara used the lengthening silence to remind herself to say as little as possible. She didn't need Ethan's, or anyone else's curiosity stirred. Cal had too many connections, knew too many people. If he decided he gave half a damn about either her or Misty, he might be inclined to search for them. Not that she thought he would suddenly discover love in his heart. He simply didn't like losing...especially not what he considered his possessions.

She stared out at the scenery, fascinated by the vast expanse of land and rock formations. In some places the land looked too parched, and in general, it was on the arid side, but somehow the desolation added to its beauty. So unlike Dallas, where she'd spent her entire life. If she weren't so darn scared, this would have been a great adventure.

"How long have you lived here?" she asked, turning to Ethan.

"All my life."

"It's beautiful."

He nodded.

She waited, hoped he'd say something else. It appeared she'd have a heck of a long wait. Misty was still happily listening to her tape, even though it probably was for the hundredth time, so Sara decided to leave well enough alone and continue to enjoy the scenery.

After another five-minute stretch of silence, she asked, "How long has it been since you've seen your nieces?"

He looked startled. "Why?"

She shrugged. "Just making conversation." She sighed, and mumbled, "Sorry," before she let her gaze stray out the window again.

A minute later he said, "It's been a long time. About six years."

Sara smiled to herself. Progress. She waited another minute, then said, "How old are they?"

"Twelve and six."

Six? Only a year older than Misty. Excitement

simmered in Sara's chest. "How long will they be here?"

"Until Christmas."

He turned down a long dusty road that seemed to go nowhere, and she remained quiet, forcing herself to breathe slowly. His younger niece's company would be great for Misty, and surely he wasn't equipped to care for the two girls by himself. Whereas Sara was really good with children. And the isolation of the ranch was perfect. If Cal were looking...

Her heart started to hammer at the thought she might be able to give Misty a decent Christmas after all. Now, all she had to do was convince Ethan Slade that for the next two weeks, she was indispensable to him.

"THE KITCHEN is that way." Ethan gestured to his left. "I'll show you the two rooms the girls will be using."

"Wait a minute." She finished settling Misty on the couch with her headphones. "Can't we go peek in the kitchen? I have a feeling that's where most of my elbow grease will be needed."

"Later. After I leave." He started down the long hall, his chest tightening as he approached the master bedroom. The one that had once been used by his parents and then by him and Emily.

The kitchen, he wasn't ready to face. Emily had spent too much time there, cooking and canning and proudly gazing out at her vegetable garden. The patch of land was surely nothing but weeds now, but the memories would still be thriving.

He hadn't managed to lose the lump in his throat that had formed when the house had come into view, and the sooner he got out of here the better. "This room here—"

He frowned at the empty hall behind him, then started to retrace his steps. Where the hell was Sara?

She was standing in the middle of the family room, slowly running her hand over the intricate details of the mahogany rocker his grandfather had carved. For whatever reason, it was the only piece of furniture in the room not covered by a white sheet.

She looked up. "This is beautiful." Her gaze wandered toward the dirty windows framing a portion of the San Juan Mountains. "And the view..." She shook her head. "It's a shame no one lives here anymore."

"You can look at all this later," he said gruffly, which earned him a quizzical look. "I want to show you the bedrooms, then I have to go."

"All right." Her hand fell from the chair, and she started toward him. But then she stopped, and so did he.

"What now?"

She was staring at the stone fireplace. "Over in that corner," she said with a jerk of her chin. "Is that where you're putting the tree?"

"What tree?"

She looked at him like he'd grown a horn in the middle of his forehead. "The Christmas tree, of course."

Ethan groaned and rubbed his eyes. "I'm not getting one. We don't have any ornaments anyway."

She shrugged. "It might be fun for the girls to make some."

"No tree." He stalked down the hall without turning to see if she'd followed. But she sure as hell had better be right behind him, or...

She was. "Why not?"

He briefly closed his eyes. "Because I don't have time to find one or worry about decorations."

"I can do that."

"You won't be here."

"Oh." She drew in her lower lip for a moment, then opened her mouth, but at his warning look, promptly shut it again.

He opened the bedroom door, and musty, dusty air poured out, throwing them both into fits of coughing. Quickly, he brought his attack under control, but Sara seemed to be gasping for breath.

"Are you okay?"

She nodded, coughed, then gasped.

He circled his fingers around her upper arm and drew her away from the room. She felt tiny, fragile, where her arm should have been more meaty.

Peanut butter and crackers.

Was that her staple? Was that all she could afford?

He kept his hand wrapped around her arm, not sure if she needed him to steady her, as he opened a window. Frosty air snaked down the hall, but at least she'd stopped coughing.

She took a couple of shallow breaths and shifted her arm. He got the message and released her.

"Okay?" he asked, ducking his head to get a better look at her face. Her color was high and her eyes too bright but she quickly nodded.

"I'm fine, really." She took a deeper breath. "I had a touch of asthma as a child and occasionally I have a slight attack. Nothing to worry about," she added hastily. "I outgrew it in my teens."

The information bothered Ethan. He wasn't sure she should be doing this kind of work. "Look, Sara—"

She touched his arm, alarm in her eyes. "Please, don't withdraw the job offer." She lifted her chin. "I need the work."

Ah, hell. Why did she have to look at him with those big pleading blue eyes like that? "Wait here a minute."

He returned to the room, flipping on the ceiling fan on his way to the window. Good thing Sam had talked him into keeping the utilities turned on. Of course Sam thought Ethan would have tired of the caretaker's shack and returned by now. It wasn't that simple.

The window was old and stubborn from lack of use, but he finally managed to open it halfway. More cold air swirled through the room, but it sure beat letting the musty stagnant air suffocate them.

He went to the next room and did the same thing. On his way out to call Sara, he saw Emily's sewing basket sitting on the oak dresser. His heart thumped as memories of them sitting by the fire sliced through him as cleanly as a knife through pudding.

She'd loved working with her hands, and she'd loved Christmas. Around July she'd always started sewing and knitting presents. He still had every sweater she'd knitted him. They were all in boxes he never opened.

"Ethan?"

He didn't know how long he'd been standing there staring, when Sara's troubled voice drifted to him. Silently he cleared his throat as he saw her in the doorway. Her nose was still red from her coughing fit, and so were her cheeks. She looked about sixteen. "I was trying to air out the rooms."

She sniffed. "It's better already. I take it this is the other room you want me to get ready?" She started to cross the threshold, but he stepped forward, causing her to stop.

"Let's give it a few more minutes to air out. I'll show you where the bathrooms are." His tone was apparently too abrupt because she looked at him with a mixture of concern and fear, and took a wobbly step backward.

He didn't have the words to fend off her fears, so he merely gave her a wide berth as he passed her. "I think one bathroom will be enough for the girls," he said as he peered through the open door just down the hall.

The walls were covered with a startling pink wallpaper, the tile floor only a couple of shades lighter. It was one of two guest bathrooms, and Emily had insisted on the colorful decor. He'd truly hated it the first day she unveiled her handiwork, but she'd said bright colors boosted her spirits. And that had been enough for Ethan.

He thought he heard Sara chuckle, and he glanced over his shoulder. She smiled, her teeth perfectly straight and as white as new snow.

"How old did you say your older niece is?" she asked, a sparkle of amusement in her eyes.

"Twelve. Maybe thirteen."

"I wouldn't count on one bathroom being enough."

He rubbed the side of his neck. "Why not?"

There was that twinkle in her eyes again. Made her look real pretty. "Because girls that age notoriously take hours getting ready."

"Ready to do what?"

"Anything."

Ethan shook his head. It was going to be a long two weeks ahead of him.

"If you're going to have your own bathroom, the two girls could probably work it out sharing one." She ducked past him to get a look inside, and a subtle fragrance drifted up to him. From her hair. It smelled like roses.

"Well, this certainly is an interesting color." She stepped inside and swiped the wall. Her palm came up brown, and she wrinkled her nose. "Wow! How long did you say it's been since anyone lived here?"

"Six years." Six years, one month and three days. "The girls will have the bathroom to themselves. I live in the caretaker's place."

She turned to him with wide eyes. "You're leaving them alone here?"

"No. My—" He caught himself, paused, then gestured with his chin toward the east pasture. "Sam, the Double S foreman, lives in the bunkhouse nearby. Along with about half a dozen ranch hands."

"Are they all men?"

He nodded slowly.

"You can't do that."

Ethan sighed. "I'll see the girls every day."

She put a hand on her hip. A slim but nicely rounded hip. "That isn't the point."

"I know every single one of those men. There isn't a thing to worry about."

"But they're only children, you can't—"

She stopped abruptly at Ethan's warning look. He wasn't about to argue. He didn't know if it was because he hadn't dealt with the persistence of a woman in a long time, or because it was this woman in particular. But she sure was getting under his skin.

He did feel a little bad, though, seeing the alarm narrow her eyes and the way her body tensed. Made him wonder about her husband, and why she was traveling alone, or why she needed the job. He wouldn't ask. It'd likely invite questions about himself.

She rubbed a hand up her arm and gave him a measuring look. "If it would help, Misty and I could stay awhile. No charge, of course. Just room and board would be fine."

"I appreciate your concern, ma'am," he told her, "but I believe I have everything covered."

"Of course." She gave him a tiny smile. "I guess I'll get started."

She led the way back to the family room, her walk not as spry as before, and he couldn't help wondering about her again. Not that it was any of his damn business. Or that he wanted to get involved.

"I was thinking I should start with their bedrooms

first,'' she said over her shoulder. "Then the bathroom, next the kitchen and save the family room for last. If I'm not finished before they get here, they can at least settle in while I tackle in here.''

He stood beside her at the edge of the family room and frowned. "You don't think you'll finish in time?''

Her brows shot up as she surveyed the room. "I wasn't expecting quite this much...neglect.'' Quickly, she turned to him. "I'm not complaining. And I'll get it done....''

"You're right.'' He laid a hand on her arm in reassurance, and her gaze raised to his, her eyes too big and too blue. Immediately he withdrew his hand and swallowed. "There's a lot to do. I'm going to get one of the men to help you.''

She blinked, and fear flickered in her eyes. "What men?''

"One of the ranch hands.''

"Oh.'' She rubbed her palms together, then dragged them down the front of her jeans. "Why don't we see how far I get by tomorrow first? No need to interrupt their work schedule. The owner might not like it.''

"He won't mind.'' She still looked tense, so he added, "We can decide tomorrow evening. But you have to promise me you won't lift anything heavy.''

A shy smile curved her lips. They were naturally peach-colored, and he felt a stirring where he damn well shouldn't. "I promise,'' she said.

"Okay.'' His tone was gruff, and she stiffened. "I'll get out of your hair. You need anything, go to the bunkhouse and ask for Sam. He's a good man.''

She was about to say something, but her daughter sat up from her lounging position on the couch and yanked off her headphones. Sara hurried over to her. "Is the tape finished, honey?"

The little girl nodded, her gaze glued to Ethan.

"Do you want to listen to another one?" Sara brushed the child's bangs out of her sleepy eyes. "Or you can listen to Baby Beluga again."

"I'm hungry, Mommy," Misty whispered softly.

Ethan heard it anyway.

Sara's cheeks pinked and she leaned down to say something in the girl's ear.

He looked away, not wanting to intrude. He scanned the dusty white shapeless mounds and realized he couldn't recall what the furniture under the sheets looked like. Panic tightened his throat, gripped his chest.

How could he forget? This room had once been a haven for him, for both of them. He didn't want to forget any part of their life together. Not a second. Ever.

It was a mistake to come here. Damn that Jenna.

"Ethan?"

He heard Sara calling to him and realized he was already at the door. His hand tensed on the knob. "I'm going out to the truck and get the cleaning supplies." He slid her the briefest glance, and saw her pass a cracker to Misty before he stepped outside.

It took only one trip to unload the supplies. He left them on the porch, then drove away at breakneck speed before the demons picked up his trail.

Chapter Three

It had been dark for nearly an hour before Sara took her first break. In spite of the open windows and the brisk December air whipping through the house, she felt damp and clammy from exertion. Long tangled strands of hair refused to stay within the piece of elastic she'd tied around her curly mop, and they clung to her damp, flushed cheeks and neck.

And still she saw little progress as she surveyed the bedroom. Sighing, she sank onto the only chair in the room, a soft overstuffed club-style monstrosity, and prayed she could get up again.

Originally, she'd thought the amount of money Ethan had offered her was generous. Not anymore. Not with the king-size headache she had from inhaling dust and the insistent ache plaguing her lower back. She was beginning to doubt she'd even be able to make the place presentable in two days. Actually, a day and a half was more accurate. The girls would be arriving early afternoon the day after tomorrow.

A crocheted doily had fallen from the dresser and without leaving the chair, she scooped up the lacy snowflake-like piece for a closer inspection. It was finely made, by hand as far as she could tell, and although at first glimpse it appeared old, Sara guessed it was more recently made. At least in this decade, when women were usually too busy to spend the kind of time required for such fine craftsmanship.

Another mystery. The house had tons of them. Like the newer add-on off the back bedroom. The house was already huge, but the owners had added yet another room. Off the master bedroom, she figured, not having seen the inside of it. Forbidden territory, according to Ethan.

The add-on alone wasn't strange. Many growing families found the need for additional space. But there was no sign that children had ever lived in the house. And then there was the owner's abandonment. Very strange.

She tossed the doily back onto the dresser. More dust filtered into the air. Sighing, she pushed to her feet. She had far too much work ahead of her to be sitting here, wondering about things that were none of her business.

After taking a peek to make sure Misty was still napping, Sara decided to work in the kitchen for a while. She really did need to develop a plan. It was maddening the way she went from one room to the other for a mop or a rag, then randomly began a new task without completing the one she'd left.

She checked her watch and decided to give herself one hour in the kitchen. That way they'd at least have a decent place to sit and eat dinner. Even if it *was* only peanut butter and crackers. She turned on the water in the sink and gazed out the window. In the distance, the tops of the San Juan Mountains were already covered with snow.

Directly in front of her, a man walked slowly toward the house. Tall, slim, broad-shouldered, for a second she thought he was Ethan, and her pulse leaped.

Her reaction surprised her. A flash of disappointment that it wasn't him downright annoyed her.

The man didn't seem in any particular hurry, and she watched as he stopped to toe a square of weathered concrete sidewalk that led to the back door. Appearing satisfied with its condition, he continued toward the back stoop.

She held her breath, waiting to see if he had a key or would knock.

He knocked, and she exhaled.

"Ms. Conroy?"

That he knew her name alarmed her. Instinct told her that he was probably the foreman or one of the hands, especially judging by his worn boots and battered Stetson, but underestimating Cal in the past had cost her, and she wouldn't be foolish again.

Another knock…a pause…then, "Ms. Conroy? I'm Sam Singleton, the Double S foreman."

She quickly unlocked the door and opened it. "Sorry. I had the water running and didn't hear you."

He removed his hat. He didn't look anything like Ethan. His hair was lighter, his eyes blue and he was clean-shaven. Besides, this man smiled. "Ethan told me you'd be here cleaning the house up some. I just wanted to let you know you're not alone on the property."

"I appreciate that, Mr. Singleton."

"It's Sam."

She nodded and smiled back. "I'm Sara."

He was looking at her funny. "You just get into town?" he asked.

"A little over a week ago."

A thoughtful frown pulled his brows together. "And Ethan found your name on a bulletin board?"

She nodded, amused at the irony that he seemed to be wary of *her*. "He said references weren't necessary."

Sam's frown deepened. "What?" then he looked slightly embarrassed. "I wasn't questioning you, it's just that Ethan doesn't show up around here much, and I was a little surprised he—" He gave a small shake of his head. "Never mind. You just holler if you need anything."

"Thank you." She was about to say something when he set his hat back atop his head and turned to go. "Wait, Sam, I, uh, was kind of wondering something."

He stopped and eyed her cautiously.

"About Ethan—"

Caution gave way to alarm, and then his entire expression shut down. "Sorry, ma'am, that topic is off limits."

"I was just…" She lifted a hand in helplessness. "I figured since you were his boss…" A strange look crossed his face. "Never mind."

She wasn't going to get anywhere with him. She'd received the same reactions in town. First there was the look of alarm, which turned guarded then blank. The only thing missing in Sam's reaction was the trace of pity she'd seen in everyone else's eyes. If anything, Sam looked protective.

He started to leave again, stopped and said, "If you're worried about his character, you won't find a more honorable or loyal man. Anyone in town will confirm that." He gave her a brief smile, touched the rim of his hat, then sauntered off without looking back.

Sara leaned against the doorjamb, trying to temper her curiosity. She told herself it was valid to be inquisitive about her employer, especially since she was scheming to stretch two days into two weeks. But she knew better. There was more to her curiosity than making sure he wasn't Jack the Ripper.

Something about him drew her, stirred an instinct to reach out and help in some way she couldn't fathom. It was a dangerous impulse. One that had already landed her in a hellish marriage. She shuddered at the thought, then ruthlessly pushed it aside, and plunged her hands in some warm soapy water.

Tonight she'd give the kitchen a cursory cleaning, enough to at least make it sanitary. Tomorrow, after the bedrooms were in top shape she'd— A burst of melodic chimes gave her such a start she splashed water down the front of her shirt and on her sneakers. It took her a second to realize it was the doorbell. She shook the water from her hands then dried them on a rag on the way to the front door.

Misty sat up, rubbing her eyes. "Mom?"

"It's all right, honey." Sara gave her a reassuring smile, then went to the window and inched back the drapes. She had only a partial view of the front porch, but she couldn't see anyone.

It couldn't be Sam. He wouldn't come around to the front door when he knew she was in the kitchen. It was probably Ethan. But he had a key. Though he probably wouldn't use it out of respect for their privacy.

With her hand on the knob, she called, "Who is it?"

No answer.

Her pulse and curiosity both going berserk, she opened the door a crack. No one was there. Her gaze drew to a brown wicker basket sitting on the porch. It held a bundle wrapped in a large red-checked napkin.

She stepped outside and stooped down for a look. Under clear plastic wrap was a roasted chicken, biscuits and cole slaw. Her gaze snapped up, but still she saw no one. Was this from Sam? But why not hand it to her?

Stepping off the porch and into the yard, she squinted toward the bunkhouse—and caught a glimpse of Ethan's blue pickup as it fishtailed in a cloud of dust down the gravel drive.

SAM SWUNG the saddle off Thunder, used his sleeve to wipe the sweat off his brow, then watched Ethan approach. His friend didn't come to the ranch much. Sam figured he could count on one hand the number of times Ethan had been here in the past six years. He hoped this was a good sign. It wasn't right for a man to isolate himself the way Ethan did. Too much grief and sadness had a way of keeping a man from being whole.

"Hey, Ethan, I got your message late yesterday.

I was riding the north pasture. Looks like we've got two miles of fence-mending ahead of us.''

Ethan stopped and stroked Thunder's neck. The soft-eyed gelding pushed his face forward for Ethan to rub. ''Have you seen her?''

Taken aback by the question, Sam tried not to show any reaction. He'd expected a comment about the fence-mending. ''Sara? Yeah, I went over and introduced myself. Pretty little thing.''

Ethan shrugged. ''Doesn't matter. As long as she gets the job done.''

Hope swelled in Sam's chest. The hell it didn't matter. He saw the flicker of life in his friend's eyes. ''Where'd you find her?''

''An ad on Manny's bulletin board.''

''Good timing. When do the girls get here?''

''Tomorrow.''

Sam straightened. ''Tomorrow?'' He lifted his hat off his head, and mopped his forehead. ''Tomorrow.'' He grunted. ''Isn't that just like Jenny? No notice. No consideration.''

''She calls herself Jenna now.''

''Tough.''

Ethan smiled.

Sam looked away. He'd grown up with Ethan and his little sister. Only, the last time Jenny'd visited she wasn't so little anymore, and her childhood crush on him hadn't seemed so silly.

''I need a favor,'' Ethan said. ''Can you spare one of your men?''

Glad to have his thoughts pulled away from Jenny, Sam studied his friend. Normally he would have automatically said sure, or you're the boss, but something told him to hold back. "What for?"

"To help Sara."

"Clean?"

Ethan shook his head. "Mostly do the lifting."

"Why can't you do it?"

The flash of fear in Ethan's eyes was like a ray of sunshine to Sam. "I'm busy," Ethan said, shaking his head. "You just said we have fence that needs mending."

"Not right away."

"What about Bobby? Can't you spare him?"

Sam massaged the back of his neck, frowning, in a show of concern. "I already gave him time off to go see his folks up in Albuquerque for the holidays."

"And Gus? What about him?"

"He's driving a herd to South Fork."

Ethan rattled off a few more names. Sam made more excuses.

Ethan exhaled, long and slow. "You've got to have somebody."

"Nope. Afraid I don't." The more panicked Ethan looked, the better it made Sam feel. It was good to see some life in his friend again. Damn good. "Unless..."

"Yeah?" Impatience and hope animated Ethan's face.

Sam shrugged. "I suppose I could give her a hand. Maybe she'll be grateful and have dinner with me." He winked, then hid a smile at Ethan's sudden frown.

"I thought you were busy."

Sam shrugged again. "Shouldn't take long. Anyway, I sure wouldn't mind her company."

Ethan silently stroked Thunder's neck, his brows furrowed in thought. Finally, he sighed. A put-upon sigh. For Sam's benefit, no doubt. "You're right. Shouldn't take long. Guess I can handle it."

"You sure?" Sam kept a straight face. "I don't mind."

Ethan flexed a shoulder, a nervous habit he'd had since they were kids. "Nah, I can manage."

Sam turned to his bucket of grooming supplies and busied himself with finding a brush before he started grinning like a village idiot. "Let me know if you change your mind."

"Thanks." Ethan sighed again. "I'd better get to the house and see if she needs me."

Sam nodded, but didn't look up until his friend's scuffed boots were headed away from the stables and toward the house. He watched his retreating form, noticing the new life to Ethan's step, and a lump swelled in Sam's throat. It was so damn good to see traces of the old Ethan. God bless Sara Conroy. Sam hoped she did need Ethan. As much as Ethan needed her.

TEN MINUTES LATER, Ethan stood on the front porch of the house to which he'd sworn he'd never return and pressed the doorbell button. If he had half a brain in his head he would've let Sam deal with Sara. But that wasn't right. Sam had carried the major burden of the ranch for the past six years. And Erika and Denise *were* Ethan's problem...

"Ethan?" Sara had opened the door, startling him

out of his thoughts. Her lips curved in a shy smile. "We just finished breakfast. Leftover chicken and biscuits, thanks to you."

She stepped aside, and he had to force his feet to move over the threshold. The sun hadn't been up long, but enough of its rays touched her auburn hair to turn the tips to gold. When he passed her, the scent of roses took some of the starch out of his knees.

"Well, what do you think?"

He looked blankly at her.

Her expression fell, and she cast a forlorn look over the family room. "Can't you see the difference?"

Ethan slowly scanned the room. All the sheets were off the furniture, the brass lamps gleamed and the hardwood floor had been polished to a high shine. "I can't believe you did all this already."

She lifted a shoulder. "It's amazing how much you can get done when there's no TV to distract you." She laughed self-consciously, the sound sweeter than pecan pie. "Come see the blue bedroom."

He let her lead the way, bracing himself for the assault of tormenting memories. But as he stepped into the room, all he saw was how cheery it seemed. The drapes had been tied back, letting the early-morning sun stream in through crystal-clean windows. Without dust covering everything, the oak headboard and nightstands and dresser looked new and inviting. Something else was different, too....

"Well? Think the girls will like it?"

He slowly nodded, trying to figure out what had

changed. "You probably didn't notice, but I swapped the comforter for one I found in the linen closet. This yellow one makes the room cheerier."

He remembered now. The other quilt was a navy blue and tan one his mother had made the year she died. Emily had used it as a remembrance.

"Is something wrong? Wasn't I allowed to go into the linen closet? You hadn't mentioned it being off limits."

Ethan looked at Sara. She was wringing her hands, her eyes dark and wary. "No, I didn't. I, uh, it's fine, Sara. The room looks real nice."

"Where are you going?" She hurried after him down the hall. He had the sudden urge to get out and breathe some fresh air.

"I forgot something in the truck. I'll be right back."

"Need some help?"

He stopped abruptly, and she nearly ran into him. He turned in time to grab her shoulders and avoid the collision.

Her wide-eyed gaze lifted to his. "I'm sorry." Her breathy words fanned his chin.

"My fault. I didn't signal."

She laughed softly, and he was amazed that he'd actually attempted a feeble joke. When her gaze lowered to the slim shoulder he still cupped, he quickly dropped his hand.

He stared at her, unable to remember what he was about to do. Clearing his throat, he moved back a step. "I think I'll just go—"

"You're leaving?"

The disappointment in her voice sent a flush of

pleasure through him. "Actually, I was—" He gestured toward nowhere in particular.

"Oh, yeah." She smiled. "You were going out
to get something in your truck."

"Right." He immediately headed for the door,
calling himself every kind of dumb jackass. He
wasn't some wet-behind-the-ears seventeen-year-
old. He didn't even like petite, fair-haired women.
And he wasn't in the market for a fling or anything
else. Dammit.

So why in the hell was he getting all tongue-tied
and weak-kneed? And stupid. He was being really
stupid. Maybe he ought to reconsider Sam's offer.
Let *him* make a fool of himself. Because something
about that woman would do it. Make a man do
something foolish he'd end up regretting for a long
time.

He circled his truck a couple of times, trying to
regulate his breathing. Anger more than anything
was throwing him off balance. That he could have
this physical reaction to a woman he barely knew
galled him.

Removing his hat, he lifted his face to the warmth
of the faint winter sun and closed his eyes. Maybe
he was getting all worked up over nothing. Of
course he would have a reaction to a woman. It had
nothing to do with Sara, personally. He was thirty-
six years old, for cripes' sake, hardly over the hill.
And he hadn't had any female company in a mighty
long time.

At that thought, he slumped against his truck. It
was by his own choice, he reminded himself. The
problem was, he wanted to keep it that way. But he
wouldn't be able to if Sara kept smiling at him.

Chapter Four

"On the count of three, lift your side and move it three feet to the right." Sara paused. "One, two—"

She waited a moment for Ethan to pick up his end, and when he didn't, she let go of her corner of the couch and popped her head up to see what was taking him so long.

He stood there glaring at her.

"What?" She left her crouched position and scrambled to her knees and propped her elbows on the arm of the couch. "Three comes after two. Why isn't your side off the floor?"

His gaze narrowed. "Would you please get out of the way and let me move this by myself?"

"That's silly. I'm perfectly capable of helping." She shoved away the stray tendrils of hair that clung to her damp flushed cheeks, then cupped her hands under the corners of the couch. "One, two—" No movement on the other side.

She popped up again, this time climbing all the way to her feet, and planting her hands on her hips. "Ethan Slade, you may be paying my salary, but you're making me madder than a—than a hungry grizzly bear.''

He eyed her a moment then moved to the center of the couch, muttering, ''You've never even seen a grizzly bear.''

''I heard that.'' She stepped back when he lifted the couch off the floor by himself and moved it. ''Who says I haven't?''

He didn't answer, and she hadn't expected him to. He'd barely uttered four sentences all day. She didn't know why he'd bothered showing up since it was obvious this was the last place he wanted to be. Except he was too chauvinistic to leave her to handle the moving and lifting.

Which was absurd. She could practically lift her own weight. All the forced hours of working out in the exercise room Cal had built for her was *one* thing for which she could thank him.

Arms folded, she watched Ethan mosey around the room, moving pieces of furniture so that she could get at the dust beneath them. Other than sliding her a couple of guarded looks, he avoided her gaze. Nothing new. He'd treated her like she was a wildcat he needed to stay clear of, making sure she didn't trespass or attack.

Still, she had to admit, with his help she'd accomplished more today than she'd expected. But maybe that was his plan. Get rid of her as soon as possible.

That thought stole some of her thunder. Staying here through the holidays would be so perfect. Misty had been quietly occupying herself with the limited toys Sara'd been able to bring, but she knew that wouldn't last. However, a six-year-old friend would be a godsend.

Sara pressed her lips together. Letting her temper get the better of her would not further her cause. Uncrossing her arms, she pasted a smile on her face. "Ethan?"

He paused, his entire body tensing as he looked her way.

Good heavens. What did he think she was going to do to him? She broadened her smile. "Would you like a cup of tea?"

His gaze touched her mouth, lingered for an unnerving moment, then skittered away. "No thanks."

"Water?"

He shook his head.

She sighed. Loudly. He still wouldn't look at her. "Ethan, have I done something to offend you?"

He looked now, his gaze narrowed, his brows furrowed. "No."

She waited for him to ask why. He went back to moving furniture.

Sara mentally counted to ten, then picked up the dust mop and attacked the floor with a vengeance. When she'd finished one side of the room, he quietly began returning the chairs and tables to their original places. She continued working, countering his silence with her own, until he put the brown leather club chair in the corner near the fireplace.

She opened her mouth to tell him it couldn't go there, but a perverse streak of rebellion changed her mind. Instead, she leaned the dust mop against the stone hearth and dragged the chair three feet to the left.

Dusting her hands together and standing back to see if she'd cleared enough space for the Christmas tree, out of the corner of her eye, she caught Ethan scowling at her.

"What do you think you're doing?" His words were low and deliberate.

She turned a smile on him. "Me?"

"Are you that bound and determined to hurt yourself?"

"Come here."

His glare melted and he blinked. "Why?"

She scooted around the couch and approached him, amazed when he actually took a step back, fear flashing in his eyes. "I'm not going to bite." She stopped directly in front of him and flexed her right bicep. "Feel this."

A startled laugh lightened his expression. "What?"

"I'm serious. Feel this."

"Why?"

Impatient, she grabbed his hand, but she wasn't prepared for the slightly rough texture of his fingertips and her thoughts skittered in a shocking direction. Quickly, she composed herself, then brought his hand to the small but firmly carved muscle she had developed over the years.

Astonishment flickered in his eyes.

"Not bad, huh?" She released his hand almost as hastily as he pulled it away.

His gaze met hers, held it for a moment, and then he slowly, wordlessly shook his head and took two steps back.

"Ethan." She cupped her hips and stomped a foot. "Would you tell me what's wrong?"

"Nothing." He picked his hat up off the table near the door. Their gazes met again, and something in his eyes sent a shaft of heat through her. "I just remembered something I forgot," he mumbled, and took off for his truck.

"Damn coward," she muttered, then took a deep breath, relieved he was gone.

ETHAN THREW his hat down on the passenger side of the truck, picked it up and threw it down again. He'd forgotten how stubborn females could be.

Not Emily, though, he amended. She was as sweet-natured as they came. He pictured her sitting near the fireplace on the brown club chair, knitting or crocheting, smiling and humming as she worked. A cross word never fell from her lips. The one time he'd heard her say darn she'd been horribly embarrassed.

Relief and guilt warred within him. This was the first time he could remember thinking about her without a knife slicing through his heart. Time would lessen the pain and grief, his friends and neighbors had told him. He hadn't believed them. Hadn't wanted to believe them. Emily deserved more from him.

His gaze strayed toward the house, his thoughts toward the little spitfire inside. She may look small and fragile, but she had muscles in her arms that would put some of his ranch hands to shame. Still, her biceps weren't all that big, more unexpected because she looked so feminine with all that flowing red-gold hair and full wide mouth, and it got him wondering about where else she might have a muscle or two that would surprise him.

Disgusted as he was with his thoughts, he couldn't let go of them. Sara's smile had somehow dug a groove in the replay area of his brain and kept bushwhacking him when he least expected it. Like last night in the shower, and then after he'd hung his hat for the night. What he had to do was get the hell out of here. Go string some fence. Chop wood. Take Jet for a long ride. The stallion hadn't been exercised today.

And when Ethan was finished, he'd go straight back to his shack in his own corner of the world and stay put until it was time to pick up the girls. He glanced at his watch. Erika and Denise would be here in less than twenty-four hours and he'd have more than he could handle. Sam could give Sara a check out of the ranch account and Ethan wouldn't have to see her again.

He patted his shirt pocket for his keys. Then his jeans pocket. No keys. He patted his shirt again. What in the hell had he done—

"Mr. Ethan?"

He turned abruptly at the sound of Misty's soft voice. She immediately turned pink and half hid behind the white picket gate to the sidewalk.

Oh, hell. He cleared his throat. "Yeah?"

"Are you coming back?"

His gaze rose over her head. Had Sara put the girl up to this? "Does your mom know where you are?"

Her eyes got big, and she shook her head.

"She's not going to like you being out here alone."

A shy smile lifted her tiny lips. "I'm not alone. I'm with you."

Something in her tone and face tugged at him. Something akin to trust. It pierced a corner of his ice-encased heart, shattering it, the pieces melting faster than he knew how to respond. "Well, I'm not sticking around, so you'd better go inside."

He expected her to bolt for the house. He didn't want her trust. Didn't deserve it. Emily had trusted him. Look where it got her.

Obviously he hadn't sounded as gruff as he thought. Misty's expression didn't even waver. "When are you coming back?"

He passed a weary hand over his face. "I don't think I am."

Alarm widened pretty blue eyes so much like her mother's. "Who's going to bring us dinner?"

Surprised, Ethan frowned, then started to chuckle.

"What's so funny?" She wrinkled her nose. "It's not polite to laugh at somebody."

"I'm sorry."

The corners of her mouth started to lift again. "Mom says you're a nice man. You're not really a grouch. Just maybe sad about something."

Ethan's humor fled. What did Sara think she was doing analyzing him?

From inside the house, Sara's panicked voice called out for her daughter. Misty spun toward the sound, then she looked back at him. "Don't tell her I was out here, okay?"

He nodded.

"Promise?" She was halfway down the sidewalk but she stopped and waited for him to answer.

"Promise."

"Then cross your heart," she said, walking backwards toward the house.

Using his index finger, he made an X on the left side of his chest where his heart should have been. At least someone still thought he had one.

As soon as Sara saw Ethan's truck in the drive that evening, she let go of the drapes so he couldn't see her waiting. At least she assumed the dust that had been kicked up belonged to his truck. The dusky twilight hampered her vision and easily camouflaged the dark-colored pickup.

She was glad Misty was still changing into her pajamas, just in case Ethan put up a fight. Not that he'd win. Sara pushed back her sleeves, then leaned against the door and listened.

A minute later she thought she heard the truck's engine and possibly the door opening. She didn't hear it close, but that didn't surprise her. The coward had probably left the driver's door open and the motor running.

When she heard the steps to the porch creak, she flung open the door. The astonished look on Ethan's face was priceless. He'd been just about to set a picnic basket on the porch, but he immediately straightened.

"Here," he said and tried to hand her the basket. She didn't take it. "What's this?"

He shrugged. "Supper."

"How nice." She opened the door the rest of the

way and stepped back. "Come in. I'll set an extra place at the table."

He rolled a shoulder, and tried to pass her the basket again. "I'm not staying."

"Why not?" She tilted her head to the side and eyed him quizzically. What in the heck did he think she wanted from him other than a job?

"I have things to do."

"I see." She straightened her back. "Thank you, Mr. Slade, but we don't accept charity."

He put his booted foot in the door when she attempted to close it. "What are you talking about?"

She eyed his boot meaningfully, and he drew it back. "I thought you were bringing some food to share so that we could all sit down together, not make a charitable deposit."

"A what?"

"I've already made something for our dinner, but thank you, anyway."

He still didn't move so she turned around and headed for the kitchen. As she passed the hall, she called to Misty that dinner was on the table. Behind her, she heard Ethan mutter a curse.

She bit back a smile and kept on going.

When they got to the kitchen and all that was on the table were crackers and cheese, a nearly empty jar of peanut butter and a cut-up apple that was beginning to brown, her bravado faltered. Embarrassment swelled in her chest until it blocked her throat. What kind of mother did he think she was? He wouldn't know that eating like this for an entire month would still be better than staying under Cal's cruel and controlling thumb.

Without a word, Ethan set the basket in the center of the table, sat down and started unloading the food. A ribbon of steam spiraled up from the slab of ribs he unwrapped, and the pan of baked beans was also still hot, judging by the way he handled it. Two large ripe tomatoes and a bag of baby carrots had been carefully kept away from the hot stuff.

When he pulled out the lattice-topped pie, her stomach rumbled indelicately. Horrified, she turned away and got out another plate and silverware.

"Wow!" Misty walked into the kitchen, her eyes wide and focused on the table. "I'm having seconds."

Sara smiled, but the ache in her chest grew. She should be the one providing this meal for her daughter. "Maybe you'd better have firsts first, huh? After you say hello to Mr. Slade."

Misty looked shyly at him. "Thanks, Mr. Ethan."

He winked at her, a rare smile curving his mouth, and a flutter replaced the ache in Sara's chest. Then she watched in amazement as Misty, who was normally shy around men, took the chair closest to him.

Putting Ethan's plate and silverware in front of him, Sara nodded to her daughter. "Let's see your hands."

Misty held up both palms.

Sara vaguely acknowledged they were clean. Standing so close to Ethan, she'd gotten a strong whiff of a musky pine scent that made her understand her daughter's attraction to the man. When his gaze warily lifted to her face, she knew she'd lingered too long.

Unnecessarily, she reached over and fussed with

the stack of napkins. "This looks great." Her voice sounded high, unnatural. She cleared her throat. "Did you make it?"

"Only the beans."

"Oh." She sat down and lamely passed the plate of crackers to Misty, who looked at her as if she were insane. "The drinks," Sara said abruptly and started to jump up.

Ethan laid a hand on her arm. "Here." With his other hand, he brought out a carton of orange juice.

Sara stared numbly at it. He hadn't released her arm yet, and his warmth was doing strange things to her thought process. "Glasses," she said weakly.

"I'll get them." His hand trailed away from her and her entire body tightened.

Sara swallowed. How pathetic. A man treated her with decency and she turned into a disgusting puddle of need. She helped Misty fix her plate, noticing that Ethan had gone unerringly to the cabinet where the glasses were kept. He took three down and was about to turn toward the sink when he realized she'd already washed them all.

Their eyes met and she quickly looked away.

"That's enough, Mom."

Sara stared down at Misty's plate. She'd dished up enough food for three linebackers. Quickly, she put the filled plate in front of her own chair and fixed Misty a new one.

Ethan sat down and glanced at the mound of food. She thought she saw a twinkle of amusement in his eye, but he said nothing, just silently poured three glasses of juice.

"Thank you," she said, and Misty immediately echoed her.

They ate in silence for the next few minutes, Misty eating so fast that Sara had to put a restraining hand on her arm twice. Sara's own appetite had dwindled as she worried about what Ethan must be thinking.

She wanted to explain to him she really wasn't a bad mother, that her daughter had a good appetite, that she really wasn't starving…that she was far better off today, homeless and poor, than she was a month ago, living in the Conroy mansion.

Sara reminded herself often enough. It was essential in order to fend off the self-doubt that had been so intricately molded and sculpted by years of criticism and belittlement.

Swallowing, she slid Ethan a glance. He chewed slowly, glancing up to give Misty a fond look before he took a sip of juice. There was no censure in his expression. He wasn't sitting in judgment, finding them both lacking. He wasn't Cal.

As if he sensed her stare, his gaze connected with hers, and his mouth slowly curved in one of his rare smiles. The lump in her throat grew so large she thought she'd choke. She picked up her glass and sloshed juice all over the oak table.

She scooted back to avoid getting the front of her shirt splashed, and Ethan promptly reached over and soaked up the spill with his napkin.

"God, that was so clumsy. I'm sorry." She used her own napkin to dab at the table.

He gave her a strange look. "It was an accident. Forget it."

She nodded unevenly and looked at Misty.

Her daughter's eyes had widened on Ethan, then she looked at Sara. "Daddy would have yelled all the way to Houston, huh, Mommy?"

Sara stiffened. "Finish your dinner or you don't get any pie." She stared down at her own plate and picked up her fork, not wanting to meet Ethan's eyes or answer any questions.

After another lengthy silence, she chanced a peek at him. He was staring at something on the table where he'd mopped up the juice, his expression melancholy. For an instant she feared she'd stained the wood, but all she could see were several lines carved into the oak. Initials perhaps, she thought, squinting for a better look.

"I'm finished. Can I have pie now?" Misty took a noisy slurp of juice.

Ethan's gaze stayed glued to the spot on the table, his face so bleak it gave Sara a chill.

"Wait a few minutes and we'll all have some together, okay?"

Misty made a face and slumped back in her chair. "Mr. Ethan, why aren't you eating?"

He blinked and slowly turned to look at her. Clearly still preoccupied, he didn't respond right away. Blinking again, he gave her a faint smile. "I bet you're ready for some of that peach pie."

Misty giggled. Even she realized Ethan hadn't been paying attention. "Peach? I don't think I've had that before. Have I, Mommy?"

"No, I don't believe so." Sara got a knife from the drawer and proceeded to cut the pie, aware the entire time of Ethan's mood swing.

He wasn't grouchy or surly or unpleasant in any way. In fact, he said nothing else. But the sadness in his eyes stirred her curiosity and carved a path straight to her heart.

"Ethan?" She offered him a generous slice of the dessert.

He stared at it for a few seconds, then shook his head and scraped back from the table. "None for me. I need to hit the road."

"Already? We haven't had—it's early."

He gave her an odd look.

"I mean, I haven't even shown you how much progress I've made."

A sad smile lifted his lips as he got to his feet. "The house looks real nice, Sara. You've done a fine job."

"I wasn't fishing for a compliment." She set the plate on the table, then dragged her palms down the front of her jeans. What she did want was an offer to stay. For another twelve days, anyway.

"I know that. All the same, the place looks nice." He carried his plate to the sink and didn't look at her when he added, "I'll ask Sam to give you a ride back to town tomorrow, while I'm picking up the girls. He'll have a check for you."

"Oh." She stood, glancing at Misty who was busy getting peach pie all over her face. "Ethan, have I done something wrong?"

The startled look he gave her should have been enough reassurance. "No." He shook his head. "No. I just—you've done everything I asked. And more. In fact, you'll find a bonus in that check."

"That isn't necessary." She picked up her plate,

no longer interested in dessert. "We had a deal. I simply fulfilled my part." She'd obviously sounded more curt than she intended, judging by the look of dismay on his face. But she was tired of being told she'd never measure up, then dismissed with a credit card and permission to go shopping.

"Can I have more pie?" Misty asked.

"No, but you may go wash your face."

"But, Mom..."

"Now, Misty."

Her daughter recognized the tone, immediately excused herself and headed for the bathroom. Sara continued to clear the table without looking at Ethan. "If there are any other instructions, I guess Sam will let me know."

"Sara?"

She sidestepped him to get to the sink, already regretting having thrown the bonus offer back at him. Damn her stubborn pride. She could use the money for Misty's Christmas presents. Not to mention a roof over their heads since Ethan didn't want them staying.

"Sara, could you just listen a moment?"

"I'm listening." She started filling the sink with warm sudsy water.

"Could you stop and listen?"

"Not really. I have a lot of work to do yet tonight."

He placed his hands on her shoulders and when she stiffened, he immediately released her and stepped back. "I'm a little nervous about the girls coming tomorrow, so don't take anything I say or do personally."

She left her hands in the water, and slid him a sideways glance. ''I can stay and help.''

He took two more steps back, his expression tightening. ''I don't think that would work.''

She sighed and resumed washing the dishes. So much for not taking things personally. ''It was just a thought,'' she muttered.

When he allowed too much silence to pass, she glanced over her shoulder. He stood near the table, a dirty dish in his hand, but he was just watching her. Their eyes met and the longing she saw there made her breath catch.

He set the dish back on the table. ''I really have to go. Sorry I can't help with the cleanup.'' He picked up his Stetson, and fidgeted with the rim. ''Thanks for everything, Sara. And good luck.''

Without waiting for her to respond, he hurried out the back door.

Chapter Five

Ethan checked his watch. The train was late, and his patience was a quart low. He hadn't slept worth spit last night, and he didn't expect tonight would be any better.

The girls were coming, and Sara was leaving. When had his simple life gotten to be such a bitch?

He checked his watch again. He'd been hoping to get back to the ranch before dark, but it didn't look like that would happen. Why couldn't they have come on a bus? Buses stopped at Sedina. The closest train station was several hours from the ranch.

Another round of *Silent Night* started over the intercom system, and Ethan turned up his jacket collar and headed outside to wait. The cold was preferable to both the crowd of waiting passengers and the never-ending refrain of Christmas carols.

Christmas, or any holiday, hadn't mattered to him one way or the other. But Emily sure had loved Christmas. Every year, a minute after the Thanksgiving meal ended, started the tradition of dragging out the ornaments and choosing the perfect tree.

He half smiled at the memories, then with a jolt

of surprise, realized some of the pain of remembering was gone. Unease crawled down his spine. This wasn't right.

A whistle signaled the arrival of a train, and he automatically checked his watch. This had to be the girls, which meant it was possible they could get back to the Double S before dark. Before Sara left…

The direction of his thoughts annoyed him, coiled a knot of fear in his gut, and he pushed back inside the station, erasing the craziness from his mind. It was better for everyone that she left. That he didn't see her again. Confusing things had started swirling inside his head—disruptive things.

When the train came into sight and slowed to a stop, his heartbeat sped up, and he realized he was kind of excited about seeing the girls. He wondered if Erika still looked like Jenna.

Nearly half the passengers had detrained and met up with the people waiting for them before he saw two girls step from the train onto the platform. Except…they couldn't be the ones. The ages were right, but…he squinted for a better look, and then muttered an oath. The older girl had purple hair. And a ring in her nose.

"Uncle Ethan?"

He stared as both girls approached him, the taller one was grinning, while the shorter one hung back, wary curiosity creasing her smooth little-girl face.

"Uncle Ethan, right?"

The older girl stopped, her smile faltering, and snapping him out of his stunned silence. He nodded. "Erika?"

Her lips lifted again and she moved toward him,

looking so much like her mother it brought a lump to his throat.

Awkwardly he opened up his arms to her.

She gave him a big hug, and the growing lump edged out any words he had planned. "This is Denise," she said, grabbing her sister's sleeve and pulling her forward. "Come give Uncle Ethan a hug."

Denise jerked away from Erika's hold. "You're not the boss," she muttered, eyeing Ethan.

He couldn't help but grin as he held out a hand. She didn't look a thing like Jenna, but she sure had her temperament. "You sound just like your mom, you know that?"

She gave him a quizzical look, and warily slid her hand into his. "But Erika looks like her."

Her fingers and wrist were so tiny and soft he didn't know if he wanted to let go immediately or hold on forever. "Yup, she does. But you have her personality."

Denise finally pulled away. "How do you know?"

"Because she's his sister, doofus." Erika rolled her eyes. "How do you think?"

Denise glared at her. "Mom told you not to call me names."

"And she told you not to be a baby."

Denise opened her mouth to retaliate, but promptly shut it again when Ethan held up a silencing hand. No one said anything for a minute. They were obviously waiting for him, but he didn't know what the hell to say.

He cleared his throat and nodded toward the bags

each of them had dropped by their sides. "Is this all?"

Erika's eyes got big. "Are you serious?"

Ethan frowned. He'd figured he was.

Denise made a cackling noise. "*She* needed a whole suitcase just for her makeup."

"I did not."

"Did too, and if you don't give me back my Walkman, I'm telling Mom you put that purple stuff in your hair and that you took some of her eyeshadow."

"Yeah? Well—"

"Girls!" At the abrupt and blessed silence, he sighed and passed a hand over his face. Relief that Jenna didn't actually approve of her daughter's hairstyle was some consolation. "Can we go get the rest of your bags?"

They both nodded and exchanged glares.

He quietly picked both their bags up with one hand, then gestured them ahead. It suddenly occurred to him he ought to keep them separated, but Erika's interest in a passing dark-haired boy seemed to cool the squabble.

Ethan took another gander at the boy who was looking back to check out Erika, and gave the kid a warning stare. Hadn't Jenna said Erika was twelve? What the heck was she doing looking at boys?

"Hey, there's my bag." Denise ran up to a battered brown suitcase the porter had just unloaded. It was nearly as big as she was, but that didn't stop her from struggling to pick it up.

"I got it." Ethan easily lifted it off the ground,

which earned him a look mixed with resentment and curiosity.

They weren't used to a man helping them.

The sudden thought disturbed Ethan. Jenna had chosen to raise her children alone, shunning the ranch that partly belonged to her. He didn't understand it. Why had she preferred the hardship of single-parenthood over giving them a home at the Double S? But there was a hell of a lot he didn't understand. Like what had happened to his and Jenna's relationship, their special bond after their parents' death.

"Oh, there's mine, too." Erika hauled a larger black bag off the assembly line. One that told him he needed to make two trips to the truck.

He felt something brush the back of his hand and he looked down to see Denise tapping him with her finger. "Uncle Ethan, I can carry one of the smaller bags." An unexpectedly shy smile curved her mouth. "Maybe both small ones."

His first impulse was to decline her help, to carry the load himself. But he realized he'd done that with Jenna. And obviously it hadn't worked.

The sudden and inexplicable realization flooded his chest with a swell of emotion he couldn't handle. He took a deep breath and quickly passed Denise one of the bags before he changed his mind. "Thanks. One will be a big help."

Her pleased grin tunneled through his heart, stoked the simmering emotions he couldn't identify. Emotions he had no intention of identifying.

"I'll take this," Erika said, trying to clear the ground with the black monstrosity.

"Trade me." He held the smaller carry-on out to her.

She made the exchange without a peep, and they all trudged outside to the truck. After he'd stowed the bags in the back of the cab and got the girls seated comfortably inside, they headed for the highway. There was no way they would make it back before dark, and he decided that was just as it should be.

Sam would have already taken Sara Conroy wherever she wanted to go. And with the size of the check Ethan had instructed him to write, he hoped she and Misty would make it as far away as they wanted to be. Ethan had enough chaos to deal with, and Sara was a distraction he couldn't afford.

"How long a drive is it to the ranch?" Erika asked after they'd been on the road for about five minutes.

"Two hours."

"Are you kidding?"

"Nope." He flipped on the defroster and cleared a section of foggy windshield with his hand.

"Are we going to be on the highway the whole time?"

"Yup."

"Aren't we going to pass a town or anything?"

At the rising panic in her voice, he glanced over at her. "Why? Something wrong?"

She looked away and stared straight ahead.

"Erika? What's wrong?"

Denise issued a loud, put-upon sigh. "She has her period."

Ethan blinked, then stared at the road. Had he heard right?

"Shut up, doofus."

"What?" Denise huffed. "That's what you told me."

He slowly chanced a look at Erika. Her face had reddened, but when she caught his gaze she shrugged. "I think I need something. This is my first time."

Ethan swallowed, then stepped on the gas. He hoped he wasn't too late to catch Sara.

SAM WAS a nice guy and Sara liked him, but she'd never actually seen anyone move slower than molasses. She understood the phrase now.

Glancing at the kitchen clock, she figured she could forget about getting to town before dark. Checking back into the motel wasn't a problem, but she wanted to get Misty fed and settled in at a decent hour.

She dried the last of the dishes she'd washed and placed them back in the cupboard. With the extra time she had while waiting for Sam, she'd managed not only to finish cleaning every room on Ethan's list, but she'd washed everything in the cabinets. Not that she'd minded. Especially after receiving the check Sam had given her from Ethan.

His generosity staggered her. The job had been undeniably hard, but he'd paid her triple their agreed-upon price. Not to mention how well he'd fed them. She knew he couldn't make much money himself, and she felt guilty taking it. But every time Misty brought up Christmas, the guilt lessened.

She hung up the dishtowel, wiped down the counter again, then looked at the clock on her way to the living room to check on Misty. It suddenly occurred to Sara that Ethan might return before they left. The idea made her palms grow clammy. It was clear he didn't want her here, and she didn't look forward to facing him again.

Especially after the dream she'd had about him last night.

Fragments of the fantasy drifted into her brain and warmth flooded her belly. How she could even think about a man after what Cal had put her through boggled her mind. But it was a dream, after all, nothing conscious. And Ethan was a fine-looking man.

She shook away the disturbing thoughts and hurried to the living room. Earlier Misty had been busy coloring a picture of Rudolph in her Christmas coloring book but she'd nodded off. Thank goodness she wasn't hungry. Sam had brought over a snack along with the check and his apology for taking so long.

Sara had been tempted to ask him about the initials carved in the oak kitchen table. Ethan's mood had plummeted about the time he noticed them, and the fact that they were ES really had her curious. Made her wonder about Ethan's relationship to the owner of the ranch.

Her thoughts started hopscotching until the distinct sound of Ethan's truck coming down the gravel drive made her heart thud, and she hurried to the front window. He was driving fast. Too fast.

After he parked the truck, he jumped out without waiting for his nieces and strode up the walk so hastily, Sara automatically stepped back. He had the oddest look on his face, something close to panic, and fear settled on Sara's shoulders. Had something happened to his nieces?

He threw open the unlocked door. As soon as he saw her his expression relaxed. "Am I glad to see you!"

Her heart picked up speed. "Sam's been tied up," she said, at a loss for anything else. "He's going to run me back to town in a half hour."

"Oh." He took off his hat and shoved a hand through his hair right through the ridge left by the Stetson. "The thing is—" He cleared his throat. "I want you to stay."

She blinked, unprepared for his announcement. "Here?"

"Well, yeah."

"For how long?" Her heart really started racing now. Did this have something to do with caring for his nieces? Of course it did. What else would he want her for? At the possibilities, her heart all but exploded.

"As long as you'll stay. Until after Christmas?" The uncertainty in his face and voice tore at her. "Of course I'll pay you well."

Disappointment pricked her. Which was absolutely silly. She knew this request related to his nieces. Straightening, she said, "You've already overpaid me. I'll accept room and board for Misty and myself."

He shook his head, looking as though he was about to argue.

She cut him off. "That's my deal."

The girls had climbed out of the truck, and, looking nervous, he glanced over his shoulder at them coming down the walkway. "Okay. Fine."

"Oh. One more thing. A Christmas tree."

His brows drew together as he turned back to her. "You want a Christmas tree?"

She nodded, amazed to realize he even had to think twice about it. "A big one that will fill that entire corner."

He followed her gaze to the stone fireplace. The nervousness was gone and he seemed subdued. "Okay."

"Can we get it tomorrow?"

"You'll get your tree, Sara," he said, briefly meeting her eyes before the girls claimed his attention.

The note of irritation in his voice startled her, and she watched with interest as he mumbled something to the older girl before he headed back to the truck and hauled out their bags.

Sara took a second look at the girl. She had purple streaks in her hair. Choking back a laugh, Sara smiled at the two kids. No wonder Ethan was in a tizzy.

"Hi," she said, holding the door open wider. "I'm Sara Conroy. And you're Erika and Denise?"

"She's Erika," the younger one said, hooking a thumb over her shoulder. "I'm Denise."

Behind her, Erika rolled her heavily made-up eyes. She sure didn't look twelve. "Hi, Ms. Conroy. Uncle Ethan told us about you. He drove like a bat outta hell trying to get here before you left."

"Really?" The hair...makeup...language. Oh,

boy. Sara didn't have to ask why Ethan was so anxious to turn his nieces over to her. "Did he tell you I have a five-year-old daughter who isn't used to hearing that kind of language?"

Erika's grin faded, and her cheeks turned a bright pink. "I'm sorry. I don't usually—" She shrugged sheepishly.

"Mom doesn't allow her to talk like that, either. She's just showing off." Denise walked in, her gaze bouncing around the living room. "Where's your daughter?"

"Probably hiding from *you.*" Erika gave her a peevish look before tossing her hair and making a U-turn toward the truck and Ethan, who didn't seem to be in any hurry to bring in the bags.

Sara sighed. "Well, she *was* asleep."

Just as expected, given the amount of noise, Misty's head popped up and she rubbed her eyes before staring at Denise in surprise. "Mom?"

"Misty, Mr. Ethan's nieces are here. Come say hello to Denise."

Excitement brought color to Misty's pale cheeks as she crawled off the couch and walked over to them. It had been a long time since she'd had someone to play with, and Sara felt a mixture of guilt and gratitude.

"Hi," Misty said softly, plastering herself against Sara's side.

"Hi back at ya." Denise grinned. "You have a cool name."

"I do?" Misty inched away from Sara.

"Yup. I never even heard it before. Wanna show me around?"

Misty nodded, then glanced at Sara.

She gave her the okay sign, pleased to see her daughter respond so well to Denise. One of Cal's legacies was stunted social skills. Too much criticism did that to a child.

Ethan stepped up on the porch juggling three bags, Erika at his heels carrying a smaller one. He looked so harassed and harried, Sara almost felt sorry for him. But they were only kids, after all. Even if one did have purple hair. She peered more closely at Erika. And a nose ring? Oh, my.

"Here, let me take one of those." Sara tried to wrestle a bag from him, but he held on tight.

"I got it," he said, then paused. "Look, I need to—would you mind—Erika needs to talk to you," he said abruptly, and then headed straight for the hall toward the bedrooms.

"Misty is showing Denise around," she called out so he wouldn't be startled.

He grunted and disappeared around the corner.

Sara stared after him, bewildered at his behavior. True, she didn't know him, but from what she'd seen, this grumpiness was uncharacteristic.

Erika didn't follow, but set down her bag and sighed. "He's freaked because I started my period."

Sara issued a short laugh. "What?"

"It's my first time, and Denise opened her big mouth. But I know what to do. My mom explained everything," she quickly added. "I asked Uncle Ethan to stop at a drugstore but he said I had to talk to you first."

A smile tugged at Sara's mouth. So that was the emergency keeping her here. "Okay, let's see, I believe I have something you can use until we get to a store.''

"Thanks.'' Erika shrugged, looking a little sheepish and shy suddenly.

Sara slipped an arm around the girl's shoulders. "You must be very excited. This is an important time in a woman's life.''

Erika shrugged again. "I guess.''

"Don't mind your Uncle Ethan. He's a bachelor and he doesn't understand certain things about women. I'm sure he didn't mean to make you uncomfortable. He probably just didn't know what to say.''

The girl smiled. "Yeah, I know. Men are like that, my mom says. But Uncle Ethan isn't a bachelor.''

Chapter Six

Ethan killed as much time as he could, setting the girls' luggage in their rooms, checking to see that their beds were made up, the closets cleared. He trusted Sara to have taken care of everything, but he wanted to make sure he'd given Erika enough time to talk to her. Coward that he was, he hadn't even warned Sara about what was coming. Of course, he figured that kind of talk was no big deal. For women.

He shuddered at the thought of what might've happened if Sara had already left. No way would he'd have known what to do. Or even if he was supposed to do anything.

He checked the heating vents to make sure they were working properly, then wandered around the room, noticing Sara's little touches, like the pink rose in a crystal vase sitting on the dresser, so real-looking he had to go touch it to find out it was silk. He tried not to think about where she'd found it—probably in a linen closet. He trusted she'd respected his wishes to stay out of certain rooms.

A burning sensation started in his chest when he

spotted the lace doilies on the nightstands. Emily had spent hours in front of the fire crocheting them. He picked one up and realized they had been freshly laundered. Sara had done that rather than store them away.

"Hi, Mr. Ethan. I'm showing Denise around."

At the sound of Misty's voice, he returned the doily and turned around. Both little girls were standing shoulder to shoulder, Denise nearly half a head taller, her hair and eyes darker than Misty's. They were both smiling, friends already, innocence keeping their lives simple. For now.

"But don't worry," Misty added solemnly. "I told her where we're not allowed to go."

Just like that, a chip of innocence was lost, and sadness coated his heart. "You wouldn't be interested in those rooms, anyway. Nothing in them."

He lied. Emily's things were still just as she'd left them in there. And memories. Too many.

"When do we get to see the horses?" Denise eyed the cream-and-pink rose wallpaper on her way to the window where she perched herself on the cedar storage box, then stared outside. "Mom says you have lots of neat horses. And cows. But I want to see the horses first."

"How about you get unpacked and have some dinner? You'll have plenty of time tomorrow to see the ranch."

"Me, too?" Misty's voice was soft, her eyes big and round. "May I see the horses?"

"Sure." Denise didn't even look back but kept craning her neck for a look at the south pasture.

A smile tugged at Ethan's mouth. Good for Jenna.

Her kids sure had self-confidence. He looked at Misty whose uncertain gaze darted between him and Denise. "If your mom says it's okay."

Misty grinned. She still had all her baby teeth, unlike Denise. "She'll say okay as long as you're there."

A sudden warmth filled him at the implied trust. And then he remembered. Emily had trusted him. Now she was dead. "You girls decide how you'll divvy up the rooms, and I'll make sure your luggage is in the right place."

"Where you going? To a fire?"

He hesitated at the door, unaware he'd been so hasty in his retreat, and looked at Denise. She'd picked that phrase up from Jenna. It had been one of his sister's favorites. "No, smarty pants. Some of us have things to do."

Denise giggled at his reply. Just like Jenna used to do. Like a pot of beef stew, mixed feelings simmered in his belly.

Familiarity. Longing. Denial. Regret. Ingredients that all made one hell of an unappetizing recipe.

"LOOKS LIKE we have to make a trip to the store." Sara opened the cupboard and reached for the glasses. She was so short that even raised on tiptoes it was a stretch for her.

"Let me get that." Ethan had just entered the kitchen and he went straight over to help her.

She didn't step aside, so he reached over her. Big mistake. The rose scent of her hair drifted up to him. The swell of her fanny brushed his thighs. It took every ounce of his control not to jump back out of harm's way and make a spectacle of himself.

He edged back slowly. It wasn't easy.

"Wow, the owners must all be giants." She smiled as she picked up the glasses he'd set on the counter, clearly unfazed by their contact. "Everything is up so high and I can't find a stepstool anywhere."

Ethan looked away. She was right. Emily had been tall with dark hair, dark eyes...so different from Sara....

That he'd even thought to compare them sent a white-hot shaft of anger though him. "We need to go to the store?" he asked gruffly. And then he remembered Erika, and his irritation deflated as quickly as a punctured balloon. "Because of?" He inclined his head in the direction of the living room.

"Erika? No, I've taken care of that already." She met his gaze with a strange intensity. "We need groceries."

He stared dumbly. How could he have forgotten *that* small detail? Briefly, he closed his eyes and sighed. "I'll bring something over from my place for tonight. Hope you don't mind roast chicken again."

"Sounds fine to me."

"Some biscuits and canned corn will be about the quickest things to go with it."

"Great." She smiled, but still had that odd, unidentifiable look in her eyes. "And, of course, there's breakfast. I don't imagine you'll get to the store before then."

"Right. Oatmeal okay?"

She nodded.

"I'll leave you the truck and money tomorrow. Then you can pick up whatever you ladies want."

The strange look was gone. Panic replaced it. "You can't do that."

"Sure." He shrugged. "I won't need it. I'll be on horseback most of tomorrow."

"No, I mean—I can't drive."

He frowned. "What?"

She tucked a strand of hair behind her ear in a purely nervous gesture. "Is the truck automatic?"

"Nope. It's a stick shift."

She almost looked relieved. "I can't drive a stick."

Ethan exhaled a sound of annoyance. The last thing he wanted to do was drive a bunch of females to the store. "Have you ever tried?"

She briskly shook her head.

"I can show you how. We can take a few runs down the drive and—"

"Are you crazy?" She planted her hands on her hips. "I'm not going to take a few practice shots and then pile three kids in and cross my fingers, hoping I don't screw up."

"Heck, I wasn't suggesting that." He lightly kicked the side of the cabinet with his boot. "I'll take you tomorrow, but if you ever need the truck for anything, you ought to know how to drive it. I'm just offering to show you how."

"Oh, well, maybe." She turned back to filling the glasses with juice, carefully making sure it was evenly distributed among the three glasses.

He felt like a heel for having forgotten something

so basic as food. The girls all had to be hungry; Sara, too, for that matter. Only he'd never heard a word of complaint out of the woman.

Damn. Something else occurred to him.

"I'm gonna go get dinner, then when I get back I'll help you clean another room for yourself. If we don't get it done this evening, maybe you won't mind doubling up with the girls for tonight."

"I don't mind at all." She turned and flashed him a strained smile. "But you don't have to stick around and help me clean. I'm sure you'd rather get home to your wife."

Ethan stared at her in stunned silence. What the hell was she doing to him? Was this her idea of a sick joke? He took a deep, steadying breath—then blindly pushed out the back door before he said something he'd regret.

THE LOOK on Ethan's face just before he'd left earlier haunted Sara the rest of the evening. Her appetite gone, she'd let the girls devour the chicken and biscuits and fruit he'd once again left on the porch after ringing the doorbell. His leaving without a word wouldn't have totally surprised her except that his nieces were here. But they were so hungry and still so excited over their trip that they hadn't commented much.

Of course, being the good smoother-over that she was, Sara had made excuses for him. Cal had taught her well in that arena.

It annoyed her that she automatically fell back into the old habit. But no more. Ethan would have to account for himself. He had no business deserting his nieces the way he had and leaving them to the care of a virtual stranger. He was lucky she was a responsible, concerned adult.

She dumped the load of dirty dinner dishes into the sink of soapy water and cocked her head to the side. It wasn't luck, really. Ethan was conscientious and responsible. Even with such a short acquaintance, she could tell that much about him. So maybe he instinctively knew he could trust her? The thought warmed her. She liked that explanation a lot. She figured she'd hold onto it for a while. Especially after years of being reminded of her ineptness.

Most of the time she'd been able to turn a deaf ear to Cal's blowhard ranting…except when he criticized her mothering ability. For some reason, in that area, his sharp tongue could always pierce her confidence.

She plunged her hands into the sudsy water, and out of the blue, Ethan's face replayed in her mind. Something had definitely spooked him earlier. At first she'd thought it had to do with her knowing he had a wife. But the truth was, he hadn't done anything inappropriate, or led her to believe one way or the other about his personal life. He'd even beat a hasty retreat a time or two.

To her shame, she had been the one to have improper thoughts about him. Even if most of them had been in the form of dreams. Which, of course, she had to replay in her mind several times over the past two days.

Still, there were inconsistencies, like why his wife wasn't caring for his nieces. Or why he hadn't taken

Erika directly home for the guidance Ethan obviously felt uncomfortable giving the girl.

Sara had been tempted to pump Erika for more information, but the child had promptly clammed up after spilling the beans about Ethan's wife. She'd mumbled something about being forbidden to talk about that and then quickly changed the subject.

Thinking over the solemn look of contrition in Erika's eyes made Sara wonder if some tragedy had taken place. Like maybe Ethan's wife was an invalid, and that's why she couldn't take care of the children. That would certainly account for his reluctance to talk about her.

Or maybe the simple truth was that it was none of Sara's business. After all, she had a daughter, yet Ethan hadn't once asked her about a husband.

Sighing, she finished washing the dishes, and instead of asking Misty to dry, Sara finished the task herself. She needed the distraction, and bless Misty's heart, she already had one. In spite of how different they were, her daughter and Denise were getting along like long-lost sisters. Just the sight of them happily doing a puzzle together brought such a joy to Sara's heart she could weep.

She'd gotten her Christmas gift early, she figured, returning to the living room to peek contentedly at the pair. And tomorrow she'd remind Ethan about getting their Christmas tree. She definitely wouldn't mention his wife again, and she prayed he wouldn't mention driving his truck. She was embarrassed to admit she didn't know how to drive. Cal had forbidden it. And the old Sara had been too young and naive to tell him to go to hell.

ETHAN SHOWED UP to take them to the store as he'd promised. At first he'd thought about taking a list and going by himself, but God only knew what kind of female things they needed. Then he'd been tempted to ask Sam to do him the favor of running them into town. More than tempted, actually, except he just couldn't find Sam.

He sat in his truck a moment, bracing himself for the onslaught of female chatter, and then slowly climbed out. He didn't get far. Denise and Misty came running out to greet him.

"Uncle Ethan!" Denise did a cartwheel halfway down the sidewalk, and then popped up in front of him. "I have another loose tooth, see?" She opened her mouth and stuck a finger inside.

He couldn't see anything but her hand. "I see. Need help pulling it out?"

Her eyes grew large and she scooted back. "No way. It'll fall out by itself."

Ethan smiled. "If you change your mind—"

Denise vigorously shook her head.

Behind her, Misty shrunk back.

"How are your teeth, Misty?"

"Fine," she murmured, and then turned and raced for the house.

"Uncle Ethan." Denise let out a long-suffering sigh. It sounded too grown up. "She's kinda shy. Not brave like me. You can't tease her like that."

"What? I was just trying to include her, squirt," he said, ruffling the top of her hair as he passed.

"Hey, you used to call my mom that."

Ethan slowed. "Yeah. She told you, huh?"

Denise nodded, giving him her toothless grin.

"She talks about you a lot." She fell in step alongside him and lowered her voice, "Remember, don't be mean to Misty. Her father was an SOB to her, and she doesn't like it when people tease her."

Ethan stopped, vaguely aware he should correct Denise for saying SOB, but anger flashed like lightning through his veins. He hunkered down to his niece's level, trying to keep his voice even, his expression neutral, when what he really wanted to do was wrap his hands around Misty's father's neck. "Did she tell you why she thought her father was mean?"

Wariness clouded Denise's eyes, and it was clear she thought she'd said something she shouldn't have. Slowly, she shook her head, but she was too young to disguise the lie in her eyes.

He exhaled softly. Of course he wouldn't push her. "Do you know what SOB means?"

She shrugged, the wariness remaining. "Kinda. I guess it means someone is mean. Mom says it when someone makes her mad. Erika says it, too, but not in front of Mom."

He pursed his lips. "So you probably understand you shouldn't say it either."

She gave a reluctant nod. "Don't tell Mom, okay?"

"Depends on how good you are for the rest of your stay." He stood, and she sighed.

"We're all ready. Shall I lock the door, or do you need to come in?" Sara stood in the doorway, dressed in a wool skirt, a yellow sweater and boots. Her hair was piled up on top of her head, and she looked so pretty it was hard to believe she was just going grocery shopping.

Of course she always looked pretty. Which was beginning to be a problem for him.

"I'm ready. Where's Erika?"

"She's with Sam. There really isn't enough room in the truck, and I was hoping you wouldn't mind when I gave my permission...."

Damn that Sam. Where was he when Ethan needed him? "No problem. He'll take good care of her. Let's go."

He gave Misty an extra smile, and then led the way back to the truck. Sara didn't seem upset about his hasty departure last night, and he was grateful. After he'd had some time to think about what she'd said, he realized Erika had probably mentioned Emily, although the girl was too young to remember much, and he suspected Jenna would have coached them to avoid the subject. Anyway, Erika obviously hadn't said too much, or Sara wouldn't have assumed Emily was alive. Or, at least, that he no longer had a wife.

He supposed he ought to set Sara straight. And even though the idea sat as well as milk gone bad, he probably would. Just not today.

After he helped both girls into the cab, he climbed in behind the wheel, and waited for Sara to seat herself. When she didn't get in right away, he leaned across the chattering girls to see what was keeping her.

A small frown puckered her brows and she'd drawn in her lower lip. When she noticed him peering at her, she made a face. "I have a tiny problem."

He raised his brows.

"I can't climb up in this skirt." She looked embarrassed. "Sorry, I forgot about how high up the truck is. I'll have to change."

Denise stopped whispering to Misty and leaned forward. "Uncle Ethan can lift you up like he did us."

Sara blinked. Twice. And stepped back. "I'll go change."

He should have let her. Instead, Ethan got out and walked around the front of the truck. "Ready?" he asked as he bracketed his hands around her tiny waist, pausing to breathe in her mysterious feminine scent, awareness shooting through him like a lightning bolt.

He knew then why he'd rushed to help. He wanted to touch her. Needed to touch her. The knowledge shocked him.

"Ready," she said breathlessly, and he realized that was the second time she'd said it.

Effortlessly he lifted her onto the seat, trying not to notice when her skirt rode up to expose one slim thigh. His insides were a mess from a heart that raced too fast and palms that were going to turn clammy at any second.

After making sure she was clear of the door, he shut it and took deep cleansing breaths of crisp winter air as he rounded the hood. He kept his gaze straight ahead to the driveway as he started the engine and adjusted the heater. It was sorely pitiful for a grown man to be feeling this way, but he had a good mind to get back out in the cold air and jog around the truck a couple of times.

He'd put in the clutch and shifted into first when Denise rocked forward and said, "I can't sit here."

"Why not?" Ethan and Sara asked at the same time.

"I'll get carsick and barf all over you."

"Eww." Misty shrunk closer to her mother.

"You sat here last night," Ethan reminded his niece.

"No, I didn't. I sat by the window. Erika sat here in the middle."

"What's the difference?"

"I need fresh air, or I'm gonna barf all—"

"Okay." Ethan cut her off, and met Sara's gaze. With a resigned smile, she checked the lock on the door. Assured that it worked, she made a motion for Denise to lift herself up. "Climb over my lap and we'll switch places."

Denise did as she was told, and Misty tried to follow, but Sara stopped her. "You can stay where you are."

"But, Mom, I wanna sit next to Denise."

The look of fear Sara slid Ethan puzzled him. And then he realized she was afraid of sitting next to him, and it filled him with so much foolish masculine satisfaction he felt like he was in high school again. So, she wasn't that immune after all.

"Misty, I said to stay where you are."

"Can I sit on your lap then?"

Ethan hid a grin as Sara tried not to glare at her daughter. "Okay," she said finally, "but if you fidget you have to sit on the seat."

"I promise I won't fi-fo—" Misty wrinkled her lightly freckled nose. "What did you say?"

Sara sighed. "Don't squirm."

"Like a slimy worm," Denise chimed in, and both girls giggled.

Shaking her head, Sara glanced at Ethan. They were close, nerve-wrackingly close, and when their gazes locked, she shifted nervously in her seat. The movement brought their thighs in direct contact, a union of wool and denim that might as well have not been there. For one long, heart-stopping moment, she froze, and he had to suck in a breath at the ridiculous pleasure her nearness gave him.

A second later, she shifted away, putting an inch between them. But her warmth was still there, burning a need in his skin so great he knew he was in trouble.

He put the truck back into gear, but before he steered them down the drive, he glanced up.

Forgive me, Emily. But I really like her.

Chapter Seven

Ethan took the gang to the new supermarket in Andersonville. He didn't know as many people there, and he didn't need stares or whispers today. One of those big fancy stores ought to have everything Sara and the girls needed, he figured, because he wasn't fixing on going through this again.

Sitting so close to Sara for nearly an hour was pure torture. Getting thrown off five broncs in a row would have been easier. He was *not* looking forward to the trip back.

Okay, maybe a little, he thought with pure disgust.

After a walk over to the hardware store for some number ten nails, he'd spotted a barber shop and gone in for a trim and shave. Foolishly he'd worried he'd taken too long, but when he returned to the store, he found they'd only made it halfway through the aisles.

"Hey, Uncle Ethan," Denise spotted him and called out before he could make himself scarce again. "Come here."

Trying not to show his reluctance, he uneasily

strode down the hygiene aisle toward them, wondering what the heck they wanted him for.

Sara was busy reading a label but she looked up and smiled at him. Her eyes widened and lit up. "You got a haircut."

He rolled a shoulder. "Yeah, I was overdue."

"Take your hat off and give us a better look."

Oh, brother. "It's just a haircut," he muttered. "You almost done here?"

"Almost." Her smile broadened. "He looks handsome, doesn't he girls?"

He edged back. "I'll see you all at the front of the store."

"Wait, Uncle Ethan, I wanna show you something."

He started to balk, but then he saw Misty watching him, waiting to see what he would do. He half smiled and hunkered down in front of her and Denise. "Yes, ma'am, what can I do for you ladies?"

They both giggled.

Denise held up an audiotape. "After I get a visit from the tooth fairy, I wanna come back and buy this, okay?"

He frowned and then caught Sara's hand signal before he'd said anything stupid. Right...the tooth fairy. He remembered now. "Tell you what, how about I buy it for you as a welcome present?"

"Really?"

"Yup." He stood. "Misty, you pick out something, too. And then you two choose something for Erika."

Misty's eyes lit up.

Sara noisily cleared her throat. "It's awfully close to Christmas to be buying gifts, don't you think?"

"No," Denise answered.

Sara lifted a brow at her, and Denise giggled, then remained silent. "May I talk to you a minute, Ethan?"

"Now?"

She gave him a bland look as she walked past him a few feet. The girls went back to studying the assortment of goodies in their miniature shopping cart, and he had little choice but to follow Sara.

"We have to discuss Christmas," she said in a whisper as soon as he joined her.

He stepped closer in order to hear better and her scent rushed him. He took a deep breath to steady himself. It was the worst thing he could do.

"Are you listening to me?"

"Uh-uh."

His frankness startled a laugh out of her. The gaze he settled on her set alarm off in her eyes. "Well, will you?"

He flexed his shoulders, and tried to distract himself by thinking about how many cows had strayed yesterday. Problem was, hanging around with cows and horses all the time probably accounted for his juvenile reaction to her feminine scent. "Sure."

"Okay." She breathed in and the way her sweater hugged her nicely rounded breasts made him forget about the cows again. "When are we buying their presents?"

"What?"

"Presents. You know, for Christmas. Obviously

we can't shop today because they'll see us, and we only have a few—''

"Hold it. You said you wanted a tree."

Her eyes narrowed. "Your point is?"

"You didn't say anything about presents."

"Ethan Slade, I know you can't be that thick-headed."

"What?"

"They're little girls. They're going to expect presents. From Santa Claus. From us."

He sighed. "Can't we just give them money?"

She rolled her eyes toward the ceiling.

"It's good enough for the tooth fairy, for cripes' sake," he muttered, and she smiled.

Not fair. If she kept smiling like that, he would agree to anything. Dammit. He focused his attention on the girls.

"Come on." She touched his arm to get his attention back. "On Christmas morning you'll be more excited than they will when they open their presents."

He doubted it. "All right. Let's talk about it tonight after dinner. After they're in bed."

Alarm went off in her eyes again. "Won't you have to get home?"

"We can't talk in front of them."

"No," she agreed, glancing their way, worrying her lower lip. "Okay, as long as you don't have to get right home."

He frowned. "You know something I don't?"

"I don't think so."

"Okay, then. Tonight." He checked his watch, glanced at the already-full cart. It occurred to him he should offer to help push it. "Shall we meet at the cashier's stand in twenty minutes?"

She looked at the list she held in her hand. "Can we make it thirty?"

He nodded, shoved his hands in his pockets and without another word, headed for the floral department. Emily liked daisies and wildflowers, but since it was winter, he figured she wouldn't mind some store-bought carnations.

IT WAS RIDICULOUS for Sara to be so nervous. But the evidence of how rattled she'd become was there. After nearly burning the pot roast and potatoes, she almost dropped two plates carrying them to the sink after dinner.

Even the girls' constant chatter throughout the meal had gotten on her nerves. She should be grateful Misty had company, and she was. It was amazing how much her daughter was blooming under the influence of Denise's outgoing personality. Christmas was promising to be much better than Sara had dared to hope. But none of that diminished the fact that she was scared to death of being alone with Ethan tonight.

Silly, she knew. He was married. He hadn't shown any interest in her that should make her feel threatened. Unfortunately, *she* was the problem. Her inexplicable attraction to him was growing like wildfire, and she felt dreadful about it. Ethan Slade was off limits.

She finished sponging off the counter and drying her hands, then looked at the clock. He'd left as soon as he'd dropped them off and unloaded the groceries without saying another word about when he'd return. But she knew he'd be here soon. Tonight was all about the girls and he wouldn't disappoint them.

Actually, her attraction to him wasn't that puzzling at all. Every time he interacted with the girls he stole another piece of her heart. Even when it was obvious, at least to her but not to the girls, that he was reluctant or uncomfortable dealing with them, he patiently listened and was never quick to react to their childish antics.

What a huge difference from Cal. In fact, even Sara felt freer to be herself around Ethan. She didn't have to live with the dread he would jump down her throat at any minute.

Thinking she heard his truck, she leaned out the back door for a look at the driveway. It wasn't him, but one of the hands who lived in the bunkhouse and drove a similar pickup. On her way back inside, she noticed a bouquet of red and white carnations sitting in a jar of water. If that wasn't odd enough, they were sitting in the narrow mudroom between the back door and kitchen.

Had Sam left the flowers there for them? Had Ethan? That didn't make sense. The bouquet hadn't been a part of the grocery purchase, and anyway she would have seen it on the way home.

Glad to have found the flowers before they were damaged by the mudroom's colder air, she searched the cupboards for a tall glass vase and then arranged the carnations with a few sprigs of pine from the yard.

The red and white blooms looked so cheerful and Christmasy they boosted her spirits. She set them on the kitchen table, and then took a minute to admire them before going to make sure the girls had brushed their teeth.

ETHAN SAT in his truck in the soothing darkness for a good ten minutes and stared at the house. Lights were on everywhere, in the kitchen, three of the bedrooms, the den. Sara had even turned the outside light on for him.

It didn't seem fair that in just a few days the place could look so homey and inviting again. Of course, it had taken more than time. Sara's sweat had changed it from a tomb to a home. So had her personal touches. Like the Christmas wreath hanging on the front door that she'd insisted on paying for with her own money today.

He smiled thinking about Denise and Misty's excited chatter about presents and decorations all the way home from the store, and their off-key versions of the Christmas carols they'd heard while shopping.

Sara was right. The girls needed the hoopla of the holidays, and Emily would have wanted that for them, too. The woods behind them were full of pine, and tomorrow he'd chop down a tree. He had no doubt Sara would give him specific instructions on what size and type she wanted, he thought as he finally climbed out of the truck. That was a gal who certainly knew her mind.

He shook his head all the way down the walkway. Not until he knocked did he realize he'd been whistling *Silent Night*.

Sara opened the door. "Why are you knocking, silly?" She stepped aside, her smile brighter than the string of colorful lights she'd hung over the fire-place.

He looked around the room. Already she had placed odds and ends of red velvet ribbon and bows, tied around sprigs of greenery. She'd cleared a place for the tree. Obviously she expected a big one.

"What are you grinning about?" She stood close, looking up at him, her full generous mouth tilted in a curious smile.

He hadn't realized he was grinning.

"No." She tugged on his arm. "Don't stop. You have a nice smile."

He grunted, flexed a shoulder. Why was she standing so close? "Where are the girls?"

"Denise and Misty just got into bed. Erika is still in the bathroom doing God knows what. Are you going to give me your jacket, or not?"

Ah. He quickly shrugged out of the fleece-lined denim jacket, and she took it and moved away.

"I just made fresh coffee if you'd like some," she said, her voice slightly muffled coming from the closet.

"Sounds good." He noticed her half-filled cup sitting on the butler's table beside the couch. "I'll warm yours up."

She closed the closet door and smoothed back her hair. Several stubborn curls sprang back and spiraled against her flushed cheek. "Actually, I think the girls would like it if you popped in to say good night."

"I thought they were already in bed."

"They are, but not asleep. And Erika should be

out at any moment." She exhaled long and slow. "I hope."

Ethan rubbed his jaw. She'd been working hard, cleaning and cooking for the kids. The least he could do was say good-night to them.

He started for the hall and then hesitated. "They aren't going to ask me to tell them a bedtime story or anything?"

A stream of soft laughter flowed toward him and her eyes lit with amusement. "I don't know. Probably not, but if they do, tell them you have to keep it short because we're discussing Christmas presents. That should cool down any marathon requests."

Oh, brother. As if he knew a story fit for kids' ears. "Okay, if I'm not out in five minutes, I expect reinforcement."

Her delighted smile sent an arrow of pleasure straight to his heart. "You got it. In the meantime I'll get our coffee."

"Throw in a shot of whiskey," he muttered as he trudged down the hall, half hoping the girls were already asleep. Yet there was that part of him that wanted to hear the soft giggles that a single look their way earned him.

The bathroom door creaked open. "Hi, Uncle Ethan. I thought I heard you."

He blinked at the freshly scrubbed Erika. The makeup was gone, so was the purple hair and nose ring. On the front of her oversize nightshirt was a teddy bear. She looked so...

"What's the matter?" she asked, with a wry twist to her mouth. "I look like a doofus, don't I?"

"No." He shook his head. "Not at all. You look very pretty."

Pink seeped into her cheeks. "I do not."

"In fact, I had no idea how pretty you were. Looks like I'll have to get my shotgun out." He winked. "Make sure I keep all the boys away."

She laughed and nudged his arm with her shoulder as she walked past him. "You'd better not."

"Hey." Frowning, he followed her. "What do you mean?"

She gave him one of those smiles. The mysterious kind understood only by other women. Except Erika was too young to know about that. Dammit. Where was Sara?

"The kiddos are in here." Erika stopped at the second bedroom and leaned against the doorjamb with crossed arms. "They wanted to share a room."

He put a finger to his lips as he peeked in and adjusted his vision to the muted light of a small lamp.

"They aren't sleeping. They're only pretending."

Both girls erupted in giggles. "We are too sleeping," one of them said.

Ethan stepped into the room, a little braver now that he had Erika with him. "Then why aren't your eyes closed?"

Both pairs of lids promptly lowered. And then the giggles started again.

"Then why aren't you quiet?"

Silence. A stray giggle. More silence.

Erika waggled her fingers at him, signaling she was leaving, and then pointed down the hall before she headed in the same direction.

He nodded, amazed at how calm he felt. How easy it was to pull the covers up to their chins, to bend down and kiss each forehead.

The sweet innocent little-girl scent that filled his nostrils wasn't so painless. It made him think of the children Emily had wanted but that they'd never had. Hadn't had time to have.

"Good night, girls," he whispered, "sleep tight."

"Good night," they whispered back.

As he quietly left their room, he was surprised by a nudge of disappointment that they hadn't asked for a story. Hoping he read her correctly, he continued toward Erika's room. She was turning down the blue floral quilt when he knocked at the open door.

She looked up with a slight frown. "Have I been here before?"

He'd hoped she didn't remember. She'd been about five the last time Jenna brought her back. "Why?"

She shrugged. "Sometimes something will look familiar."

He kept his expression carefully noncommittal. "You were here with your mom about six years ago, before Denise was born."

"Oh." Shrugging again, she plumped the pillows. "I didn't think I'd like it here. But it's kinda nice."

"Good. I'm glad." The Double S had been in the Slade family for three generations. Since he would never have children, someday she and Denise would inherit all of it.

He watched her get out her headphones and then choose a CD. She nibbled on her lower lip while she was concentrating, just like Jenna always had, and he had the sudden urge to tell her this was her home, that she and her sister and mother were always welcome here.

But Jenna had made her choice to alienate herself from the Double S and he wouldn't interfere. Besides, admitting he owned the ranch would invite questions. Ones he couldn't yet handle—especially if they came from Sara.

He didn't know why she'd popped into his head. This had nothing to do with her.

"Uncle Ethan?"

He glanced at Erika, and was taken aback again by how different and young she looked without all that strange stuff she'd been wearing.

"Mom talks about you all the time. Why do you suppose we don't come visit more?"

Shoving a hand through his hair, he considered diplomacy. But only for a second. "Guess I don't have to tell you how stubborn us Slades are," he said, and a knowing smile lifted her lips. "And sometimes maybe I was too pushy a big brother."

Erika looked genuinely startled. "She said you were the best."

Something flared inside Ethan. Hope tangled with doubt, intertwined and flamed. "I tried." God, how he'd tried. But he'd failed them both. Jenna and Emily. "You'd better get some shut-eye now."

She gave him a patronizing smile. "It's still early. But I'll just stay here and listen to my CDs."

"Right." He shifted, uncertain as to whether she was too old for him to kiss on the forehead.

Relieving him of the decision, she walked up,

rose on tiptoes and kissed his cheek. "'Night, Uncle Ethan."

"Good night, honey."

He heard her door close softly as he retraced his steps down the hall. Sara was sitting on the couch in the den waiting for him.

He glanced at the mantel clock she'd somehow got working again. Almost fifteen minutes had passed. "Traitor."

"What?" She laughed.

"What happened to my reinforcements?"

She lifted her chin. "I knew you wouldn't need any."

He took the brown leather club chair across from her. "You were wrong."

"Right." Smiling, she poured the coffee. "Sugar?"

"Black."

She passed him the mug. "Can we get our tree tomorrow?"

"I'll work on it."

"Ethan…" The way she drawled his name in warning made him dread what came next. "Christmas comes only once a year. If you don't have time, maybe the girls and I can—"

"I'll cut one down tomorrow."

"Thank you." She was all smiles again, giving his heart that jittery feeling. "I was thinking it should go over there by the fireplace. What do you think?"

"Fine."

"You didn't even look."

"Sara." His warning tone didn't seem to faze her. "I'm going to get your tree."

"And help us decorate it, right?"

He took a long sip of coffee. "What did you want to discuss about presents?"

She sighed. "Denise and Misty still—" She stopped and leaned forward, the lamplight catching golden highlights in her hair. In a lowered voice, she said, "They still believe in Santa Claus, so we have to make sure there are a couple of presents from him under the tree Christmas morning. Erika is supposed to find out what they want."

It was hard for him to think about presents or Christmas when she was leaning forward like that, the V of her blouse gaping just enough for him to glimpse a mound of creamy skin and make the blood rush to his ears. And elsewhere.

"Careful."

Her warning came too late. He started when hot coffee splashed the front of his jeans, and he quickly righted his mug. There hadn't been much liquid left, so there wasn't much damage. Just enough to prove what a damn fool he was.

"Are you all right?"

"Yeah," he muttered and stood. "I'll be right back." He didn't really need to go to the kitchen, except to collect his thoughts. So he was glad she didn't jump up and follow him.

He went through the dining room and pushed through the swinging door into the kitchen. He spotted the flowers immediately. The sight of them stopped him dead in his tracks. Were they the ones he'd—? How the hell could he have forgotten?

"Ethan?" Sara came in through the hall door. "I can wash your jeans if—" He couldn't seem to look away from the carnations, but he felt the weight of her stare. "Is something wrong?" She paused. "I found them in the mudroom. I assumed they were for us."

He finally blinked, cleared his throat.

"Who were they for, Ethan?"

"My wife." The words barely made it out of his mouth.

"I'm so sorry."

"For her grave."

Chapter Eight

The air fled Sara's lungs. She stared at him, too afraid to speak. Afraid she'd ask the wrong question; say the wrong thing. She was almost as afraid of his answer.

She must have looked pretty awful because pity entered Ethan's eyes after he finally looked at her. But his expression was still bleak, his face haunted as he moved slowly to the sink.

"Leave the flowers there. They look nice. Emily would have…" His voice trailed off, and Sara bit her lip.

"Just leave them there, Sara."

She nodded, even though he wasn't looking at her. He was too preoccupied with trying to look busy at the sink. When he finished washing his hands, he turned to her.

"It happened a long time ago," he said calmly and picked up the old percolator. "Do you want more coffee?" It took her a moment to realize she'd brought her mug, and when she finally held it out, her hands trembled. He noticed too, and their eyes met.

"I'm sorry—"

"I didn't—"

They both spoke at the same time, and then she gave him a shaky smile. He tried to return it.

"We're supposed to be talking about Christmas," he said quietly, looking down into his own mug. "I didn't mean to throw a wet blanket on things."

"I'm glad you told me."

His gaze raised to hers. "Yeah, I guess it was time."

She didn't quite understand what that meant. "Did you eat dinner?"

A faint smile touched the corners of his mouth. It didn't go any further, but it was a start. "My mama thought you could fix anything with food, too."

"I don't think that—I just figured—" She sighed in defeat. "Okay, name one thing chocolate cake can't cure."

He grunted and held her gaze so long the backs of her eyes started to burn. "All the same, I'm a little tired tonight. Mind if we continue this discussion tomorrow?"

"Of course not." She did mind. She wanted the sadness gone from his eyes and the droop out of his shoulders before he left.

But he turned to leave and panic swelled within her. "Ethan?"

He stopped, his expression full of reluctance.

She clutched the mug so tight she half expected it to shatter. "We will see you tomorrow, won't we?"

"I promised you a tree."

"I know, but—"

He doubled back toward her, jetting her pulse into the next century. When he stopped right in front of her and lifted her chin, her heart pounded so erratically she thought her life was over.

"I'll be back, Sara," he said, and lowered his face. His lips barely brushed her forehead, and then he stepped back.

He smiled then, before he left the kitchen.

Sara didn't move until long after she heard his truck speed down the driveway. Her body was numb, her thoughts racing.

Nothing had changed, she reminded herself over and over again as she washed out the percolator and measured the coffee grounds for tomorrow. She was still just his employee, here temporarily, trying to pull Christmas together for his nieces. Heck, he'd even kissed her like she was one of the girls.

She chased away the disappointment over that reminder, and told herself again that nothing had changed.

BY THE NEXT afternoon, everything was topsy-turvy. Mere change would have sounded good to Sara. But this was utter chaos. The cookies she'd made with the girls had burned, and Denise had the sniffles, and in her crankiness she had irreparably tangled the popcorn and cranberry strands that were to be part of their decorations. When Sara had tried to make a fresh batch of popcorn, nothing popped.

She dumped the charred kernels into the trash and bit off a curse just as Ethan walked in the back door. She spun toward him in surprise. The lift of the left side of his mouth told her he'd heard what she started to say. Heat stung her cheeks.

"I understand you're having a bad day." He shrugged out of his jacket and hung it on the hook near the door. At her quizzical look, he added, "I saw Erika outside. She told me to come in at my own risk."

Sara huffed. "Her disposition hasn't been the sunniest either."

He said nothing and went straight to the coffeepot, the beginning of a smile touching his lips. "I have something outside that should cheer you up."

"You brought the tree?" She raced to the window but she couldn't see anything. "You'd better not be teasing me. Did you bring it?"

He set down the mug he'd just filled, then walked toward her and all the day's blunders disappeared. Placing his hands on her shoulders, he turned her around and walked her out of the kitchen, down the short hall to the foyer. He released her and opened the front door.

Leaning against the white porch railing was a huge pine. It had to be at least nine or ten feet tall. The branches spread out to make a perfect shape. This tree was not found by accident. He'd had to look long and hard for something this perfect.

"Oh, Ethan." She brought her hands to her mouth to keep from blubbering. "It's beautiful."

"What's the matter, Sara?" Concern shadowed his voice and eyes.

Embarrassed, she waved a hand at him. "Nothing. It's just so—" She swallowed. "Have the girls seen it?"

"Erika has."

"Let's bring it inside and set it up in the corner before I call the other two to see it."

"Yes, ma'am," he said, his smile reaching his eyes for the first time Sara could recall.

"Ethan?"

He hesitated and looked at her.

"Thank you."

He seemed about to say something, but then just nodded. "Close the door for now so you don't freeze. I'll let you know when I'm ready to drag the tree inside."

"I'll help you."

"I made it this far. I can handle it alone."

She wanted to argue that two people would make the job simpler but something told her to let it be. "Okay. I'll open the door as soon as you holler."

She ended up not closing the door all the way, but left it ajar, so she could peek at him wrestling the tree up the porch steps. Was this how Ethan always handled situations? Alone. Not wanting any help or companionship? Had his wife's death done this to him?

"Ready," he called out, and she immediately swung the door wide open.

The place of honor was cleared and waiting, and she hurried to the corner where she'd set a bucket of stones to hold the tree up.

He half carried, half dragged the tree inside, then frowned at the bucket. "You think that's going to be heavy and deep enough to hold it up?"

"I think so. Anyway, we can at least try."

Looking skeptical, he nevertheless hoisted the tree

up to clear the top of the bucket, and then slowly dropped the trunk into the opening she'd left for it. Quickly she dumped more stones around the thick trunk, being careful that it was wedged in tight.

Before he even let go of the top, she knew it wouldn't work. The tree immediately started to fall toward the fireplace. He caught it before it did any damage. So quickly, in fact, she suspected he hadn't released it altogether.

"That's okay," he said. "I think I know how we can fix this. Mind holding onto this for a moment?"

"Of course not." She took his place, and then watched him disappear outside, only to return in seconds with a hammer and two pieces of wood.

An odd sensation made her feel as soft and gushy as a toasted marshmallow. He probably had known it wouldn't work, but he hadn't belittled her or her idea the way Cal would have done. Ethan simply tried her way. And spared her feelings.

Watching him work silently, she wondered why he and his wife had never had kids. He was so good with them—patient and kind and caring. But she guessed she'd never know the answer to that, or the other dozen questions about Ethan that had churned inside her head most of the night.

"I think this will take care of it." He stepped back to view his handiwork. "Sara, you can let go now."

"What?" She blinked, snapping out of her trance, then moved back alongside him. The tree cleared the ceiling by about a foot and stretched out as far as the bookcases. "It's so perfect. Ethan, the girls will be so excited." She caught his amused look. "Okay, so I'm excited, too. I admit it."

He chuckled and slid an arm around her shoulders, as if it were the most natural thing to do. She stiffened in surprise, and he pulled away with a startled look.

Sara felt the burn of embarrassment spread across her face, sorry she had reacted to his touch. Regret already darkened his eyes. She knew he'd meant nothing by the gesture, that it was probably pure impulse, but she didn't know what to say without making matters worse.

"That tree ought to hold up just fine." He'd already started backing away. "If it looks like it might lean some, give Sam a holler and he'll straighten it right up for you."

"Aren't you going to help us decorate it?"

He made a sound of disbelief. "I've got more work waiting for me than I can handle as it is."

"Then will you at least come back for dinner?"

"Can't say for sure." He made it to the door, checked the crowded coatrack, and then must have realized he'd left his jacket in the kitchen because he headed that way.

Sara followed him. "You have to eat. Unless you have a date."

He shrugged into his jacket, eyeing her with confusion, and then amusement when he saw that she was teasing. "That's right. With a heifer named Elsie. You got a problem with that?"

"No, sir, but if Elsie doesn't feed you, I will." She gave him a big smile and, when his gaze lingered too long on her mouth, this time she didn't act like a silly schoolgirl. She stared back, her smile in place.

"You wouldn't be making some cornbread, would you?" His darkened gaze rose to meet hers, and she slowly nodded. "I sure wouldn't mind having some of that ham and black-eyed peas I saw you put in the cart yesterday."

She moistened her lips. "You can have anything you want."

At his sharp intake of breath, a thrill shot through her. He hadn't mistaken her meaning. And God help her, but she hoped she knew what she was doing. Maybe it was because with the girls in the back rooms, she knew she was safe, but if Ethan showed the slightest sign he wanted to kiss her, she'd welcome him.

She took a tentative step toward him. He seemed wary, but at least he didn't back away. He just kept watching her, desire mounting in his face, making her heart pump faster as she took another step. Heat warmed the inside of her belly, then spread lower. Her breasts grew heavy, needy.

He still hadn't moved or said anything, and suddenly she lost her nerve.

She stopped a couple of feet in front of him, and lifted a shoulder in a feeble shrug. "Need something to help keep you warm in the saddle?"

His nostrils flared slightly, his gaze nearly devouring her. She opened her mouth to explain she meant a thermos of coffee or hot chocolate, but he closed the short distance between them and, cupping her elbows, pulled her toward him.

His lips probed gently, and he seemed in perfect

control, but when she flattened her palms on his chest, the tension and restraint she felt radiating from his body told a different story. The knowledge excited her, and she pressed closer, until her breasts rubbed against his lower chest. The pleasant friction stirred a moan in her throat. Ethan chased the sound with his tongue.

Somewhere in the foggy distance she thought she heard the girls giggling. Maybe it was her conscience, maybe it was real, but in any case, she broke the kiss.

Reluctant to let her go, he framed her face with his hands and continued to shower her chin and jaw with kisses and nibbles. Her hands slid down from his chest. She encountered something hard. Behind his fly. She promptly pulled away.

Oh, God, what was she doing?

"Ethan, the girls." Breathless, heated, excited, she didn't know if he'd even heard her, or if she'd actually spoken aloud. But then he stopped, his breath a jagged shadow on her skin.

He briefly closed his eyes as he moved away, inhaling deeply as he straightened. "Sara?"

"It's okay, Ethan. I just didn't want to alarm the girls if they walked in." She took one of his hands, so large and roughened from days of honest work, and sandwiched it between hers.

"I didn't mean to get so carried away."

"I did."

One side of his mouth lifted a fraction. "That should keep me pretty warm."

She frowned and then blinked when she remembered what had started everything. "I was going to offer you a thermos of coffee.'' With a shaky laugh, she released him and moved to the sink. ''The offer still stands.''

When she looked back, her eyes were immediately drawn to his impressive arousal that even the thick denim couldn't hide. Her mouth went dry, and she turned back to the sink and filled a glass with water.

She finished it off in three gulps, but the dryness remained. After setting aside the glass, she started rummaging through the cabinets. ''I know I saw a thermos in one of these—''

He'd come up behind her and ran his hands up and down her upper arms. ''Don't be nervous,'' he whispered. ''Nothing happened. We won't let one small slip in judgment change things.''

His heat penetrated right through her green wool turtleneck sweater. His arms might as well have been wrapped around her she felt so cocooned and warm and safe. Involuntarily she leaned back against him.

He hesitated before slipping his arms around her, crossing them over her chest, hugging her to him. ''I don't want you to feel awkward around me.''

''Is that what this feels like to you?'' She laughed softly.

After a moment of silence, he withdrew his arms, then turned her around and lifted her chin so that their gazes met. ''I don't want you to feel pity, either.''

She widened her eyes in outraged denial. ''That never crossed my mind. If you want to know the truth, I was relieved to find out you weren't married.''

Her bluntness shamed her, and she instantly regretted what could be construed as a reference to his widowed status. But he didn't seem upset. He obviously knew better, because if anything, he looked pleased.

''What about you, Sara? Can I assume you're not married?''

''Divorced.''

''Mind if I ask how long?''

She sighed. ''Two months.''

That information didn't set well with him. She doubted he realized it, but he even took a step back, nervously flexing a shoulder.

''It was over between Cal and me long before we signed the papers,'' she said, shrugging. ''I stuck around longer than I should have because of Misty, and a couple of other reasons I don't want to go into.''

''Fair enough.'' He had more questions. She saw them in his eyes. But he wouldn't ask, she knew, because that would leave him wide open.

''I'm twenty-seven,'' she volunteered. ''I know I look younger.''

He seemed a little surprised—and relieved. ''That you do.''

She waited for him to tell her how old he was. He didn't, although she felt fairly certain he was in his mid-thirties. ''Well, I'd better get to work on those black-eyed peas and cornbread if we want to eat supper on time.''

Ethan pursed his lips, and stepped back so she

could get the cast-iron skillet out from one of the lower cabinets. "Maybe we should reconsider my joining you and the girls."

"Why?" She used the back of her hand to swipe an errant strand of hair off her face and to get a good look at him. "I thought you said nothing happened…that things wouldn't change."

"You're right. I did."

Uneasiness stiffened her shoulders. "Sounds like you changed your mind. Did I do something wrong?"

"Of course not." He looked quizzically at her, and it struck her that she always seemed to be asking him if she'd done something wrong.

It was a difficult habit to break. When she was with Cal, he'd criticized her for doing nothing right. Darn it. She knew better.

Shrugging, she turned away. "If you think you shouldn't come back tonight, no problem. I'm sure we'll have leftovers. You can take them home with you tomorrow. I assume you'll come by to see Denise and Erika, at least."

"Sara?"

"What?" She wouldn't look at him, but crouched down again to root through the lower cabinet.

He patiently waited until she'd located a small pot and a pan for the cornbread. She wished he'd just leave. Instead, he helped her up, his hand warm and firm around her arm until she got to her feet.

When she stubbornly refused to look up, he tilted her head back by nudging up her chin. "You want to know why it might be best I don't come back tonight?''

"No."

He smiled. "Because darlin', I'm not sure I can keep my hands off you."

Chapter Nine

Ethan worked on stringing the three holes in the south pasture fence until after dark. He told himself Sam would have a fit if one more calf strayed because Ethan had been too busy socializing to get his chores done, but that was a lie. Sam was glad Ethan was finally surfacing from his six-year stupor. Too glad.

Every time Ethan asked his friend to chip in and help with the girls, he told Ethan he was too busy and to do it himself. Made a man wonder who was boss around here.

He stepped back to check the job he'd done with the fence, but it was too blasted dark to see. His stomach rumbled noisily and he wondered what time it was. One of these days he'd buy himself one of those glow-in-the-dark wristwatches. Of course he told himself that every time he headed into town, but then once he got there, he ended up in a hurry to leave.

Jet whinnied from the fence post Ethan had tied him to, making it clear he was ready to head back to the stables. "What are you complaining about?"

Ethan asked with gruff affection. "At least you've been eating."

Jet threw his head back and neighed loudly. Probably trying to remind Ethan he also could be eating right about now, if Ethan weren't such a coward.

Ethan sighed and stroked the horse's neck. "You think I'm a damn fool, don't you?"

Jet brought his head up and down as if he were nodding.

"Yeah, I know, but it's not easy, boy. Not easy at all." He untied Jet and swung into the saddle.

Sara and the girls would be wondering where he was, and though he didn't want to worry them, he wasn't prepared to face Sara yet. Or the way she was making the house look more like a home again.

It didn't seem fair that another woman could step in and take up where Emily had been forced to leave off. Even though Ethan and Jenna had grown up in that house, after he and Emily had married, they'd made so many changes, both structurally and cosmetically, that it truly became their own creation.

He'd made the changes slowly as the Double S's profits grew and they were able to afford more luxuries and the add-ons that would some day be their children's rooms.

Thinking about the babies they'd never had was a dangerous road to travel, a painful one, and Ethan quickly reined in his despairing thoughts. It was especially hard now, during the holidays, a time when Emily had always come alive. She loved baking, decorating, buying and wrapping presents and all the hoopla, which for her, generally started around October.

That's why it was hard to see Sara take over. To watch her place the Christmas tree in a spot Emily had decided wasn't right.

Ethan sighed as he gave Jet his head, knowing the horse would go directly to the stables. The ride gave Ethan time to think about how unfair he was being. Sara hadn't taken over. She was trying to make a nice Christmas for the kids—the same thing Emily would have done.

So how could the two women be so different? While Emily had been tall and dark and come from generations of good ranching stock, she'd also been fragile, timid, always depending on him to make major decisions.

Sara only looked fragile. Beneath her fair features and small-boned frame lay a will of steel, the strength to do whatever it took to provide for her daughter and keep her safe, no matter what luxuries and comforts she'd had to leave behind.

He had no doubt she'd left a privileged material life. It was obvious she was no housekeeper. Not that her work wasn't up to par, but her hands were too well maintained. And as little as he knew about women's clothes, he knew hers and Misty's were expensive. So was the gold watch circling Sara's wrist.

His gut still constricted when he thought about what Denise had told him, how Misty's father had been mean to her. Ethan didn't know what that meant exactly, and he knew enough that you sometimes had to sort out a child's tale, but obviously Sara had believed her marriage a threat, and she'd had the gumption to leave. Many women wouldn't.

He squinted up at the cloudless night sky, a favorable sign that tomorrow would be a good day for finishing up the south pasture fence. He'd work in snow if he had to, but he liked to avoid it when he could. Although he'd pretty much work in a blizzard for the next ten days if it meant staying clear of Sara.

She was too young for one thing, nearly nine years his junior. Plus, divorce couldn't be easy on a person, no matter how much greener the pasture on the other side of the fence was. She had to have a lot of crazy thoughts chasing around inside her head, and she didn't need him adding to the confusion.

Particularly since he had nothing to offer. Except Emily's house, a safe place for Sara to layover on her journey.

"What the hell...?" Ethan tightened the reins. He'd been so wrapped up in his thoughts he hadn't paid attention when Jet had wandered off the path to the shack.

Not too far up ahead was the house, all lit up, welcoming-like, a curl of smoke spiraling from the chimney through the sky, weaving through the nearly full moon.

"What are you doing, Jet? This isn't the way home."

The horse gave a noisy rebuttal, shaking his head and stomping his front hooves.

"Okay, boy, calm down." As he stared at the chimney, Ethan absently patted the gelding's neck. No way could Sara have safely gotten a fire started without the chimney being swept out. It had been neglected too long. Surely she couldn't have...

Sam.

Ethan let out a curse. It had to be his friend who'd taken care of it. Sam had mentioned the need to clean out the chimney a few days ago. Ethan had told him it wasn't necessary. Sara wouldn't be staying long.

Funny that Sam hadn't had time to do the things Ethan had asked of him, but he had time to make things comfortable for Sara.

What the blazes was Sam trying to do? Get on Sara's good side?

That thought sat as well as a burp in Sunday school, and when Ethan realized Jet had taken them closer to the house, his mood really took a tumble.

He stared at the wreath on the front door, tempted to give in and knock. But it would be plain wrong. Stupid. He could see the girls tomorrow. They'd be going to bed soon, anyway, and then he and Sara would be left alone to make small talk. Or worse.

He pulled on the slackened reins, but before he could turn Jet around, the door opened. Erika stepped outside and waved at him. She had on a long nightshirt and fuzzy pink slippers, but that didn't stop her from coming out to the edge of the porch.

"Uncle Ethan, you were supposed to be here for dinner." She crossed her arms and rubbed them against the cold. "Would you hurry and get inside before I freeze to death?"

She scampered back through the door before he could tell her he wasn't staying.

Dammit.

If he left now without saying anything, they'd think something was wrong.

He sat indecisively for another minute, and then sighed. "Satisfied, Jet? You big pain in the rear."

It didn't take much to urge the gelding toward the garage where Ethan had long ago built a modest animal shelter in the back. It had been Emily's idea. She hated when Ethan or Sam would come home for lunch on horseback and leave the horses tied up outside. An overhang hadn't been enough, he recalled with a smile, she wanted the horses to have their own garage.

He took a deep breath of cold air until his lungs burned and the memories faded. As fond as he was of replaying bits and pieces of their past in his head, he couldn't handle it right now. Not when he was about to go into the house. When he was about to see Sara.

Erika and Denise were obviously waiting for him just inside the door, and when they heard him stomping the snow off his boots, they threw open the door.

"You have to close your eyes before you come in," Denise said, "or you'll ruin the surprise."

"What surprise, squirt?" He gave his boots one last stomping.

Denise sighed dramatically. "We can't tell you that. Now, close your eyes and give me your hand. I won't let you fall."

Ethan smiled at the earnestness in her voice. Obediently he closed his eyes and held out his hand.

"I'll take your other one," Erika said. "Step up and get inside so I can close the door and not freeze my butt off."

"Your butt's too big to freeze off," Denise said

just as he blindly tackled the first step and nearly missed it.

"Look who's talking, doofus."

"Girls," Sara's soft but warning voice came from the den, and he almost cheated and opened his eyes. "Can you save the insults until you get your uncle inside without him breaking his neck?"

"Sorry," they both mumbled at the same time. And then Denise muttered something else, but he didn't catch her remark.

Better that he hadn't, he figured, judging by the sudden tense feel of Erika's hand. Denise had probably said something requiring a scolding, or at least a word or two. He wasn't much good at that. Sara was. Sometimes she got them to behave with just a look.

They led him slowly through the foyer to the den, the feel of their tiny, soft, little-girl hands in his giving him a fuzzy sensation in his chest. A hodge-podge of odors clung to the air, traces of burnt popcorn, pine, wood from the fireplace. The tantalizing aroma of cornbread he might have imagined, but his stomach rumbled anyway.

"Okay." They stopped, and Erika let go of his hand. Denise hung on. "You can look now."

He opened his eyes and saw the Christmas tree. Every branch was covered with red velvet bows, garlands of cranberry and popcorn and glittering gold stars—and glass ornaments.

Emily's ornaments.

Heirlooms passed down through her family for several generations. She loved those ornate pieces of sparkly colored glass, some painstakingly painted with miniature Christmas scenes by her great-great-grandfather.

He stared, unable to speak. Barely able to feel.

"Isn't it beautiful?" Beside him, Erika peered at the tree in wonder. "Doesn't it look like something out of a magazine? I wish Mom could see it."

Misty sat on the floor near the base of the tree, her excited eyes taking in all the details of the decorations.

"Uncle Ethan?" Denise tugged on his hand. "You aren't saying anything."

He dragged his gaze away to meet Sara's. Her smile faltered, and alarm glinted in her eyes.

"Where did you find them?" he asked.

Her brows drew together in a slight frown, and her gaze flickered to the tree. "The ornaments?"

He didn't answer but kept his eyes locked with hers.

Denise tugged on his hand again. "What's wrong, Uncle Ethan?"

"Girls, why don't you go get the marshmallows ready for roasting?" Sara gave them a strained smile. "Erika, maybe you could put on some water for hot chocolate?"

"Sure." Erika hesitated, looking anxiously from one adult to the other. "We didn't do anything wrong, Uncle Ethan."

"He knows that," Sara said quickly. "Maybe he'd like you to heat him some ham and cornbread?"

The nervousness in Erika's voice, the pleading in Sara's eyes gave him pause, and he swallowed back the anger and hurt that had started in his chest and threatened to close off his throat.

"That sounds pretty good, kiddo," he said, forcing a smile for Erika. "If you still have black-eyed peas, I could go for some of that, too."

She made a face. "We have plenty of *that* left." Hesitating, she gave them each a wary look before following the two younger girls into the kitchen.

As soon as they'd disappeared, Ethan turned to Sara, the smile gone, along with his appetite. "I thought we had a deal."

She glanced meaningfully toward the kitchen and motioned him closer. Then she sat on the couch and waited for him to join her.

He stayed on his feet, even though he knew she expected him to sit beside her. He didn't want her distracting him. Didn't want to notice the dark circles forming under her eyes that the lamplight so clearly bared.

When he looked over at the tree and saw Emily's ornaments, pain wiped any of his reticence away. Sara had trespassed. He turned back to her, waiting for her to respond.

She looked nervous. "You're probably referring to the ornaments."

He bit back the sarcastic retort that sprang to mind.

"I found them in a box in the attic." She folded her hands on her lap, but they looked a little shaky. "We stayed out of the rooms you told us were off limits."

"That's not the way I remember putting it to you."

"Oh, Ethan, I can't believe the owners would begrudge the children using their tree ornaments. They're beautiful pieces of craftsmanship. They should be displayed and enjoyed. Not collecting dust in a box."

His defenses began to mount, his temper fraying. The ornaments weren't collecting dust. They were being preserved. To Emily's memory.

"I sorted out the really delicate ones and hung them myself," Sara continued, carefully studying his face, wariness clouding hers. "The girls know they can't touch them. I'll take full responsibility."

After a few moments of stony silence, she said, "Ethan, I wish you'd say something."

She looked pale and tense, and some of his anger lessened. He thought again about Misty's account of her father, and more of his annoyance faded. Was Sara replaying old tapes right now? He hadn't meant to frighten her. But seeing the ornaments was like opening old wounds.

Sighing with frustration, he lowered himself to the opposite side of the couch. What was he going to do about this? Stay away until Christmas? Confine his visits to the kitchen?

As much as he wanted to spare Sara's feelings, looking at the ornaments still hurt like hell.

"Do you want me to take them down?" she asked quietly. "I'll think of something to tell the girls. I won't make you the bad guy."

He half smiled. He didn't expect she would. "Look, Sara, I don't want you to—"

"Uncle Ethan!" Erika ran into the den. "I remember those ornaments," she said, her eyes widening on the tree as she got closer to it. "At least these two."

His stomach churned. He'd been dreading the possibility she'd remember the one Christmas she and Jenna had spent with him and Emily. Erika had only been four at the time.

She turned to him with delight in her eyes. "Those are Aunt Emily's ornaments, aren't they?" Suddenly, she clamped a hand over her mouth, and stared at him with a mixture of fear and sadness.

He held a hand out to her. "It's okay, Erika."

She lowered hers, regret on her young face as she slowly approached him. "Mom made me promise I wouldn't bring up Aunt Emily."

When she reached him and took his hand, he realized he didn't know quite what to do. Or how to reassure her he wasn't upset with her. She took the uncertainty away by crawling into his lap and laying her head against his chest.

"I'm sorry." She sniffed.

"Nothing to be sorry about," he said, hoping he could talk around the lump in his throat. Lodged there not because of his wife's memory, but because this little girl trustingly sought his comfort. Was worried she'd hurt him. "I'm glad you remember your aunt."

"Really?" She straightened and peered at him with damp eyes.

"Really." He touched the tip of her nose. "I'm sure she's sitting up in heaven, thrilled that you're enjoying her ornaments."

Erika's lips started to curve. "I would be if I were her."

Her words startled him. The truth in them unsettled him, and he glanced at Sara. Her eyes were suspiciously bright, and her lips were pressed together.

She sniffed, and then said, "Erika, I hope you aren't burning your uncle's dinner."

Erika jumped to her feet, her head nearly taking off Ethan's chin. "Oh, my gosh."

"Check on the other two, will you?" Sara called after her when she was already halfway to the kitchen.

With obvious reluctance, Sara faced him. "About the ornaments...I'm sorry...I didn't know...."

"Of course you didn't." Sighing, he let his head drop to the back of the couch and scrubbed his eyes before staring at the ceiling. "Erika's right. Emily would want the ornaments out for everyone to enjoy."

"This is your house," she said softly. It wasn't a question, or an accusation.

"It was Emily's house."

Silence lapsed, stretched, turned stifling.

"You should have told me." Folding her arms, she shrank back against the armrest. "This afternoon when we..." she paused, took a breath, "...when we were being so honest."

"Maybe," he agreed, wishing he could erase the unhappiness on her face. Wondering if he pulled her onto his lap, whether she'd snuggle up to him like Erika had.

Another silence ensued.

"I'm sorry, Sara." He swallowed. "It's hard for me to talk about Emily."

She nodded, sympathy softening the tension around her mouth. "I'm sure it is. I don't mean to push.... I just don't want to say anything out of line, or that will bring up bad memories."

He smiled a little and shook his head. "My memories of her are good ones."

She smiled back and reached over to squeeze his hand. He turned it over so that their palms met, and he intertwined his fingers with hers. "You're very lucky," she said. "They'll always be with you."

"Lucky?" His laugh was humorless. "That's part of the problem. No one can ever replace her."

He didn't protest when Sara withdrew her suddenly cold hand.

Chapter Ten

"Uncle Ethan? Are you going to eat in the kitchen or the den?" Erika called from the kitchen door. "I can bring you a tray."

Sara drew away from him, retreating to her side of the couch. His eyes never left her, and she wished he'd look away, answer Erika, do anything but watch for her reaction.

What did he expect from her? To be glad that he wanted to spend the rest of his life grieving for his wife? Never to give himself a chance to be happy again or to allow another woman in?

"Uncle Ethan?" Erika moved toward the den. "Did you hear me?"

"Sorry, Erika. I'll be right there." His gaze stayed fastened on Sara. He waited until Erika disappeared again, and then said, "I've upset you."

"Not at all." She shrugged a shoulder. "Why would you think that?"

"Because I got carried away this afternoon, and I may have given you the wrong impression."

She forced a laugh. "This isn't the dark ages. So we got a little physical. Nothing to get worked up about.'' She stood. ''You'd better go eat your dinner before it gets cold.''

''Sara.'' He grabbed her hand when she would have walked away, and stood to face her. ''I didn't take our intimacy this afternoon lightly. And I doubt you do.''

''What do you want from me, Ethan? Do you *want* me to be upset? Do you want me to admit I can never replace Emily?'' She sighed when he flinched. ''Fine. I have no intention of ever trying to replace any woman or to be anyone but myself. I spent eight years in a horrible, stifling marriage, trying to be Cal's idea of the perfect wife. I won't make that mistake again.''

He looked stunned, then thoughtful. ''I didn't mean to— I only wanted—'' He made a sound of exasperation. ''I'm making a big mess. And to be honest, I'm not sure what I'm trying to say, because, dammit, I couldn't stop thinking about you all day.''

She squinted at him in confusion and pulled her hand away. Was he trying to give her the brush-off or not? He looked almost sorry he'd added that last surprising tidbit. ''Go eat, okay, before you make me crazy.''

''Uncle Ethan!'' Erika's voice had grown impatient.

''Coming.'' He backed towards the kitchen, but kept Sara in his sights. ''What time will the girls be going to bed?''

''In about half an hour. Why?''

''I want to show you something.'' Then he turned and strode to the kitchen.

Apprehension needled her, and she had the reflexive desire to shut herself in her room until he left. The thing was, she understood part of how Ethan felt. She didn't know what she wanted, either. The last thing she needed was another relationship. She certainly hadn't been looking for one. Ethan had been totally unexpected.

Yet something about him appealed to her at a level so deep it frightened her. She couldn't describe or pinpoint the attraction. He had many admirable qualities. Probably more than she knew. The new revelations were still sinking into her overworked brain.

She moved to the window to stare out at the scattering of lights breaking up the semidarkness over the Double S. It was a large ranch, judging by the size of the bunkhouse and stables and the distant herds and riders on horseback she'd seen when she'd glanced out the kitchen window.

Live-in ranch hands apparently weren't enough to handle the work, because every morning a parade of pickups brought more cowboys, and then in the evening they would leave again. A place this big required an enormous amount of responsibility and dedication. Ethan may have physically and emotionally removed himself from it all, but he ensured that the ranch remained operational.

No wonder the townspeople were so protective of him. She realized now that any hesitation she'd encountered when asking about him was just that—his neighbors' desire to preserve his privacy. To honor the man who'd remained honorable through personal tragedy and grief.

She smiled when she heard the girls laughing in

the kitchen. No doubt over some antic Ethan used to entertain them. The kind and gentle way he treated them melted Sara's heart every time. Even when he seemed so uncertain and obviously out of his depth when it came to dealing with three little girls, he was patient and thoughtful.

All those reasons that drew her to him were obvious attractions. But there was still something more she couldn't define. Something deeper, more primal.

Maybe it was simply because he was the polar opposite of Cal. A dangerous affection to have if that were the case.

She'd entered college on a full scholarship at the tender age of seventeen, horribly naive and unprepared for the masculine attention and the pressures of dating. After getting pretty serious with Jarred, another freshman, then getting publicly dumped by him the next summer, she was ripe pickings for the worldly senior, Cal Conroy.

By the end of her sophomore year, she'd been totally flattered by and infatuated with the well-dressed, smooth-talking "older man," and when he'd asked her to quit school to marry him, against her parents' wishes she'd accepted.

They'd begged her to complete her education, to use the four-year scholarship she'd been awarded for high academic achievement. But Cal had convinced her she didn't need a college diploma. That she'd have everything she needed as his wife. And like a silly impressionable fool, she'd believed him.

Misty's chattering drew Sara's attention and she turned to see the girls trooping down the hall toward the den. Denise was in the lead, as usual, yawning and rubbing her eyes. Normally they'd be begging her to let them stay up later about now. But they'd had a particularly active day and she wasn't surprised they were tired.

"Sara, do you know where my Barney tape is?" Denise asked, around another yawn.

"I know where it is," Misty chimed in. Unfortunately, she didn't look quite as sleepy as Denise. "It's with our letters for Santa."

Denise gave her a menacing look, and Misty promptly clamped a hand over her mouth.

"Oh, you've made your lists. Good." Sara smiled with relief. Misty had been awfully secretive about it this year and Sara was beginning to worry she wouldn't have enough time to shop. "Santa only has five more days to make all the toys before Christmas. If you give the letters and lists to me I'll mail them first thing tomorrow morning."

"That's okay." Denise grabbed Misty's hand and tugged her toward the hall that led to their shared bedroom. "We'll take care of it."

Behind them, Erika met Sara's quizzical eyes and shrugged. Ethan appeared behind Erika, his gaze darting between her and Sara in confusion.

Sara motioned Erika closer. "What's going on? Have you seen their lists?"

Erika rolled her eyes. "It's top secret. Denise thinks Santa might not be real and she's trying to test you and Uncle Ethan. That's all I know."

Sara groaned. "Terrific. Do you know how Misty reacted?"

"She says Denise is wrong. She knows there's a

Santa because he brings her tons and tons of cool stuff every Christmas.''

Sara cringed. Not this year. Cal and his parents had always gone overboard at Christmas and birthdays. They mistook extravagance for love.

Ethan joined them, looking a little awkward. ''So what do we do now?''

That he so readily included himself surprised Sara, pleased her, too. ''Steal their lists for one thing.''

Ethan laughed, another surprise, a rarity that startled both Sara and Erika. ''So, we're reduced to grand theft. Who's going to do the deed?''

Both women looked at him.

His eyes narrowed. ''No way.''

''They'd never suspect you,'' Sara pointed out.

''How would I know where to look?''

''Okay, I'll help,'' Erika said. ''I have a couple of ideas where they may have hidden the lists. You keep them distracted long enough for Sara and I to get a quick peek at the lists.''

Uncertainty etched two lines between his brows. ''How am I supposed to do that?''

''Just be your usual charming self.'' Sara smiled. ''You know those two adore you.''

He shot her a disbelieving look.

''It's true. Their eyes light up and they start giggling as soon as they see you.''

Ethan looked as though he wasn't sure how to digest that tidbit of information. ''Should I go try spinning them a tale or two?''

Erika shook her head. ''You have to get them out of their room.''

"Any suggestions?"

Erika started to shrug and then said, "Denise wanted to know about the different ornaments. I bet she'd like it if you explained about them." She glanced uncertainly between Sara and her uncle. "You can skip the part about Aunt Emily."

At the way Ethan automatically stiffened, Sara bit her lip. But he relaxed again, and though the smile he gave Erika didn't reach his eyes, it seemed enough to reassure his niece. "I'm sure I can keep them entertained for a few minutes."

"Cool." Erika grinned back as she headed off to embark on her mission. "I'll go get the little geeks."

When Ethan frowned at the girl's comment, Sara smiled. "And she means that in the most affectionate way possible."

"Yeah, I bet."

"Thank you for doing this, Ethan." She studied the way his gaze strayed nervously toward the tree. "Nowadays kids grow up so fast I'd like to preserve the illusion of…of…"

When she couldn't seem to come up with the right word, Ethan offered, "Happiness?"

She blinked. "That's not what I meant at all. I was talking about magic…wonder…fairy tales. Happiness never has to end."

He said nothing, but a cynical smile lifted one side of his mouth as he moved into the den and sat on the couch.

She bristled. "I think it was Abe Lincoln who said that people are as happy as they make up their minds to be. I, for one, choose to be very happy, thank you very much."

"Good for you, Sara." His expression and tone were so noncommittal she didn't know how to interpret that.

Before she could respond, the girls' chattering announced them a few seconds before they came traipsing into the den. Denise had changed into her camouflage-patterned pajamas, while Misty wore a pink ruffled flannel nightgown.

"I'm thirsty," Denise said, with a sly sideways glance at Sara.

Perfect. Sara needed a reason to disappear. "I'll get you each some water."

"Hot chocolate would be better." A mischievous smile curved her lips as she climbed up into Ethan's lap, totally surprising him judging by the way he started shifting uneasily.

When Denise put her little arms around his neck and rubbed her cheek against his, the look of pure wonder and contentment on his face made Sara's breath catch.

Misty stood beside them looking uncertain and maybe even a little wistful, and, bless Ethan, he coaxed her up on his other thigh.

"I'll get the hot chocolate," Sara said quickly, and hurried to the kitchen.

They'd already each had a mug earlier, and under any other circumstance she would have squashed that idea. But not tonight, and not just because it provided opportunity for Erika to snoop, but because it was hard for Sara to watch her daughter with Ethan.

As bad a father as Cal was, Misty loved him.

She'd constantly sought his approval, but she was too young to know she'd never get it.

And Ethan…he didn't realize it, but he craved human contact, physical touch, the knowledge that someone else cared about him. Maybe even needed him.

"I got it," Erika said, rushing into the kitchen just as Sara put the water on to boil. Her mouth in a wry twist, she handed a crumpled piece of notebook paper to Sara. "You're not gonna like one of Misty's. It's a real whopper."

Sara's heart thudded and her gaze impatiently scanned the girls' joint list, guilt starting to gnaw at her, knowing she'd see something about Cal. Her eyes widened at the second item on Misty's column.

"I told you," Erika said, leaning one hip against the counter. "What are you gonna do?"

Out of the dishtowel drawer, Sara pulled a tablet that she kept handy for jotting down grocery lists. "I'm going to copy some of these things down so you can return the list before they return to their room."

"No, I meant about Misty wanting to stay here on the ranch. I bet Uncle Ethan wouldn't care."

Sara kept her gaze lowered to the list she was creating. She knew what Erika meant. She just didn't know how to answer the girl without getting all tongue-tied or weepy. Good thing Ethan wouldn't see the original list, only Sara's version. She couldn't imagine what kind of panic Misty's innocent request would cause him.

The teakettle started to whistle, and Sara handed Erika back the crumpled paper. "I'll keep them distracted with the hot chocolate while you return this.''

''Don't forget to make me a mug. With whipped cream on top. Stealing is hard work.'' Erika grinned when Sara rolled her eyes, then disappeared to undo the dirty deed.

It wasn't easy to stay coordinated and load the tray. Sara's thoughts kept roaming back to the list, and her hands would shake. Every year Misty asked Santa for one really big gift, and then a bunch of smaller ones. Against Sara's wishes, the Conroys reached into their deep pockets, and Misty always got what she asked for and more. This year, staying at the ranch was obviously her biggie present. This year she'd learn disappointment.

Sara finally managed to assemble the mugs on the tray, along with a can of whipped cream, and carried the treats into the den. When she heard Ethan's deep rumbling voice, she hesitated long enough to listen to him describe one of the ornaments. He and Emily had received it as an engagement present, he told the girls who both remained on his lap, and then patiently explained what an engagement was when Misty asked.

How difficult this had to be for him…but he wouldn't let the girls down. Sara's hands began to tremble again and she hurried to put the tray on the coffee table.

''Mmm…that smells yummy.'' Denise was the first to scramble off her uncle's lap. ''Wow! Whipped cream, too.''

Misty eyed the tray but she looked reluctant to leave Ethan's lap. Sara had to look away.

"Do I smell chocolate?" Erika came dancing around the corner, her stockinged feet skidding on the hardwood floor.

"Oh, *now* you show up." Denise grabbed the can of whipped cream and shook it. "Everybody who was already in here gets to use this first. And if there's *any* left, then you can have some." She kept squirting the top of her chocolate with a mountain of the white concoction until Sara told her to stop.

"You're such a brat. But I don't care, because I know something you don't," Erika said with a Cheshire-cat smile as she picked up her mug.

That got Denise's attention and she opened her mouth to retaliate, but Ethan cut her off.

"All right, young ladies, I think we've heard enough name-calling and ugly talk. Don't you?" His tone was mild, his expression stern.

All three heads promptly nodded.

"Good. While you're drinking your cocoa, I want each of you to think of something you like about the others." He picked up the mug of coffee Sara had prepared for him, no cream, one teaspoon of sugar. "And then you can share it with the other person."

"Out loud?" Denise wrinkled her nose.

One side of Ethan's mouth lifted. "You have a suggestion on doing it another way?"

Denise shook her head and sipped her chocolate, her expression thoughtful as she gazed at the other two girls.

Sara stared at Ethan in surprise. When she caught his eye, she smiled, then mouthed, "Good job."

He lifted one shoulder slightly, but she could tell he was pleased with her acknowledgment.

"I'm ready," Denise said, startling everyone. "I'll go first."

Sara handed her a napkin and pointed to the chocolate and whipped cream mustache above her upper lip.

Denise swiped her face clean, then took another sip and added a new mustache, chocolate only this time. "What I like about Misty is that she never argues and lets me boss her around."

Sara and Ethan's eyes met briefly and they both bit back smiles.

Denise looked at her older sister. "Erika plays with me when I'm bored and gets me snacks when Mom's not home." A sheepish look crossed her face. "Even when I'm bratty."

Erika looked as though she wanted to comment, but Ethan gave her a warning look. He turned to Misty. "Are you ready?"

"Hey, I'm not finished." Denise set down her mug and let out a loud burp.

"Gross!" Erika scowled.

Misty giggled.

Sara sighed. "What do you say, Denise?"

"Excuse me. It was a mistake. Honest."

"Right." Erika's sigh was far more dramatic.

"Okay, knock it off." Ethan sounded cross, but Sara saw the amusement in his eyes. "Misty or Erika, who's next?"

"I'm really not finished." Denise jumped up and down. "I didn't tell you and Aunt Sara your stuff yet."

Sara stiffened. Not only had she not counted on being included, Denise had never addressed her as Aunt Sara before. Reluctantly, she looked for Ethan's reaction. He showed none, only waited for Denise to continue.

Pleased to have everyone's attention again, the girl grinned. "I like Aunt Sara because she never yells, even when she's scolding me. And she cooks really good."

Sara smiled with relief that her turn was over. God only knew what could come out of that girl's mouth.

"And she's so pretty," Denise added, with an adoring look. "Even Uncle Ethan stares at her all the time."

Chapter Eleven

Sara briefly closed her eyes and groaned softly. She couldn't look at Ethan. Or Misty. Or Erika. Sara knew her face was flaming, and there wasn't a thing she could do about it.

"My mom is the prettiest mom in the whole world," Misty said, and Sara's cheeks grew hotter.

"Okay, let's move on," she said, her voice sounding pretty feeble. When she chanced a peek at Ethan, he seemed uncomfortable too, his gaze carefully avoiding hers.

Unexpectedly, excitement jolted her. Although he'd already admitted he was attracted to her, knowing someone else could see it made the prospect all the more real.

"Uncle Ethan?" Denise turned her attention to him, and the apprehension on his face drew Sara's sympathy. "You tell nice stories and you have cool ornaments, and..." she moved toward him, a trace of uncharacteristic shyness in her demeanor, and edged herself between his legs, "...and I'm glad you're my uncle."

A slow smile curved his mouth as he leaned toward her outstretched arms. "Me, too, sweetheart."

"Mom said you were the best." She hugged him, some of the chocolate from her lip rubbing off on his neck.

He whispered something Sara couldn't hear.

"Come on, it's my turn." Erika tugged on her sister's nightshirt.

Amazingly, Denise complied without so much as a cross word. She simply climbed down and then sat on the rug near Ethan's feet.

"I'll start with Misty," Erika said. "You always have good manners, and you play fair." She looked at Denise. "Even when you're mad at me, you never tattletale, and you always defend me no matter what. I guess you're a pretty good kid sister."

Denise's grin stretched a mile wide.

Erika's gaze moved to Sara. "I want to be like you when I grow up. You and my mom. You remind me of her."

At that, Ethan's eyebrows shot up, but he said nothing.

"You didn't criticize or nag me even when you thought the nose ring was real," Erika continued. "And you let me try things my own way even when you know it isn't right. Like yesterday when I tried baking Christmas cookies." She made a face. "You just told me to consider it a lesson learned instead of yelling at me."

Sara felt her cheeks heating up, felt the weight of Ethan's stare. She decided not to look at him. She wasn't sure she wanted to know what he was thinking. Parenting was relatively new to her. She made things up as she went along, never knowing if she'd done the right thing. It felt weird to suddenly be critiqued. Especially by his nieces.

"Now, Uncle Ethan." Erika sighed, and it was hard to gauge if it was a good or bad one. "I started this trip off with an attitude, because I thought you were going to boss me around like you did my mom," she said, and Ethan flinched. "But I know you were kind of like her father in some ways, and if I did have a father, I'd want him to be like you."

"You do have a father, Erika," Ethan said softly. "You may not get to see him often, but he loves you."

She shrugged, the action indifferent, the hurt in her eyes heartbreaking. "He's married again, and he has other kids to worry about."

"That doesn't make you any less special to him. They haven't replaced you. Erika?" Ethan waited for her to look at him. "You know that, don't you?"

"I guess."

Sara's thoughts were reeling. Why was Ethan like a father to his sister? Why hadn't the girls been sent to their father's house for Christmas? It was both ironic and a blessing, really, that they'd all ended up here for the holidays, a makeshift family with nowhere else to go.

"My turn," Misty piped up. "I like Denise because she's my friend. And Erika and Mr. Ethan because they're nice to me. And my mom because she makes me hot chocolate." She yawned. "May I have some more now?"

Biting back a grin, Sara put a hand on her hip. "What do you think?"

Misty giggled. So did the other two girls.

"Okay, everyone to bed." Sara made a shooing motion with her hand. "Go brush your teeth, then I'll come tuck you in."

"We already brushed our teeth." Denise sluggishly trailed Misty.

Sara lifted a brow. "You just had chocolate, didn't you? Now, move."

Denise sighed loudly, but she kept going without another word.

"I'll make sure they brush," Erika said, and followed the other two.

Sara stared after them, thinking about how mature Erika was in so many ways. For all her teasing, she really did look out for the two younger ones. Was she typical of a child raised by a single mother? Often burdened with too much responsibility and robbed of some of her childhood?

Is that where Misty was headed? Guilt pricked Sara again, and she had to mentally pinch herself. When she'd insisted on the divorce, she'd known life wouldn't be easy. But she'd made her decision carefully, and now was no time to second-guess herself.

"Sara?"

She blinked at Ethan. "I'm sorry, I didn't hear you."

He smiled. "I know. Did you get a look at the list?"

She pulled the copy out of her pocket. "Pretty much the usual stuff. Although why Denise wants a chemistry set is beyond me."

Taking the list from her, he laughed. "I think we

can skip that one. Knowing her, she'd figure out how to blow something up.''

"You wouldn't think a six-year-old would have heard of a chemistry set.''

"Nothing about kids surprises me.''

Sara cocked her head to the side. ''Why is that?'' At his confused look, she added, ''You do so well with them, and your suggestion to share something positive was really great.''

He shrugged. ''Just seems like common sense to me.''

There was more, she was sure of it, but did she want to press him? ''Okay, if you don't want to talk about it, that's fine.''

"Talk about what?''

"Your being a father to your sister.'' Now she'd done it. Opened her big mouth after she'd decided not to push.

He snorted. ''Subtle.''

"That's me.'' She gave him a sheepish smile.

"There's not much to tell. Our parents died in an accident when I was twenty and Jenna was fourteen, which left me her guardian.''

"That's a big responsibility for a young man.''

"Yeah, well, I didn't do so hot. Jenna pretty much ran wild, wouldn't tell me where she was going half the time, then finally eloped and left town at seventeen.''

At the self-recrimination in his eyes, Sara's heart went out to him. ''I doubt her behavior had much to do with you. Being a teenager is difficult enough, and then to unexpectedly lose your parents.... How awful.''

"Anyway, that's ancient history."

It wasn't. She could tell by the pain shadowing his face. "Maybe," she added casually as she took a seat on the couch, "but Jenna obviously turned out all right because she's raised two fine children."

He frowned in thoughtful silence for a moment, and then a slight smile tugged at the corners of his mouth. "Maybe," he agreed mildly, and she figured, for him, that was something. "What about you? Where's your family?"

"My mom lives in Houston with my only sister, and my dad died two years ago. There's a seventeen-year gap between my sister and myself. I was a late baby, so I grew up like an only child."

"I'm surprised you didn't go there after your divorce."

Sticky territory. She shifted in her seat, curled her legs under her. "They have a full house. I didn't want to burden them."

"Did you grow up in Houston?"

She nodded. "I went to college in Dallas, and I've never lived anywhere else, so this is quite an adventure for me."

"Any particular reason you chose New Mexico?"

"It's new, different, and I've never been here." She waited in tense silence for him to ask more questions because it seemed clear he knew there was more to her decision than wanting a change of scenery. But he said nothing and glanced down at the list again.

"And I knew Cal wouldn't think of looking out west. He'd try Houston first and then maybe Austin.'' She sagged against the cushions, amazed at how good that felt to blurt out.

Ethan's gaze narrowed in concern as he set aside the piece of paper. ''Why would he be looking for you?''

''Because he doesn't like to lose.''

''Misty?''

''Either of us.''

''But you *are* divorced?''

She straightened when she realized where his thoughts had headed. ''Yes, absolutely, and I'm not doing anything illegal. I have custody of Misty.''

''I hadn't figured you'd done anything illegal.'' He studied her closely. ''At least not unless you had a good reason.''

Unease crawled up the back of her neck. He knew something. Had Misty talked about her father? ''My ex-husband comes from a very wealthy family, and he's used to getting his way. When he doesn't, he's not a...'' she paused, ''...a very nice man.''

Tension lined the sides of Ethan's mouth and his hands started to clench into fists. ''Was he abusive?''

''Not physically.'' She reached for her coffee. It had grown cold and slightly bitter. She took her time setting the mug aside, trying to gather her thoughts. ''You probably don't want to hear this, and anyway, like you said, it's history.''

''I want to hear anything you feel like telling me.''

She busied her hands, picking at a loose thread on her jeans. The problem was, she didn't know if it would feel good to unload, or if she would end up humiliated for being such a wimp for so many years. Heck, the embarrassment was already there, but she'd finally had the courage to leave, darn it.

She took a deep breath. "I met Cal while I was in college. He was smart, good looking, rich and said all the right things. Against my parents' wishes, I dropped out of school and married him." Shrugging, she briefly glanced at Ethan. Compassion, not censure darkened his eyes. "Everything was fine at first. More than fine, we had fun. And then I got pregnant."

He reached for her hand, both of them shifting a little closer together. "Didn't he want children?"

"He said he did before we got married. But two years later, when I told him I thought I might be pregnant, he went ballistic." She shuddered at the memory of that rainy night, the yelling, the threats, the put-downs, the first time Cal had instilled fear in her.

She stared down at the half-moon pattern his thumb was making on the inside of her wrist. His touch soothed her, pushed the bad memories further back. "He wanted me to get rid of the baby. I wouldn't do it. After that, my charming husband turned into a control freak. Actually, he'd always been controlling, but I didn't see it until much later. When I'd wanted to return to school, he squashed the idea. When I'd wanted to learn to drive, *he* decided it was unnecessary because the Conroys' chauffeur took me anywhere I wanted to go."

Sara reluctantly met Ethan's startled gaze. "That's right, I don't know how to drive. Pathetic, huh?"

He squeezed her hand. "Cal is pathetic. I think you're very brave. It couldn't have been easy for you to make the decisions you've made."

Her chest swelled with gratitude and pride. "Easier than you think when you have a child who's constantly hurt by her father's indifference. When he did pay attention to her, it was to criticize everything from her clothes to the color of her hair."

Ethan shook his head, the tension in his body radiating all the way to his fingertips. Still, he kept his touch on her gentle.

"At least his lack of concern made it easy for you to obtain custody. Otherwise, he might have bought his way through the system."

She laughed humorlessly. "Don't think he didn't try. He may not have wanted Misty, but he hates to lose even more. The only reason he relented was because I threatened to run the Conroy name through so much mud nobody would recognize it."

Admiration gleamed in Ethan's eyes and one side of his mouth lifted in a half smile. "Good for you."

"I had no choice. I didn't have any money or resources to fight him, but I knew his parents wouldn't stand for a public airing of laundry. His dad has his eye on a senate seat. Cal Senior can't afford negative publicity. Especially since he's as bad as his son."

The look on Ethan's face turned to pity, and she jerked her hand away.

"Don't feel sorry for me. I was an adult when I made my decision to marry Cal. It was a mistake. I learned, now I'm moving on. I'm only sorry Misty got caught in the crossfire."

"Okay," he said slowly, "then can I feel sorry for Misty?"

She stared at him, saw the amusement lurking in his eyes, and she started to smile. "So I'm a little defensive. Sue me."

"I had something else in mind." He reclaimed her hand again and tugged her toward him until she was practically sitting on his lap. He slipped an arm around her and gently rubbed her back and shoulders.

She closed her eyes. His hands felt good and strong and the tension began to melt from her body, only to be replaced by a new tension that made her heart go too fast and the insides of her thighs feel achy and fluttery. "What about the kids?" she whispered half-heartedly.

"What about them?"

"They may come back in here."

"Number one—we're not doing anything wrong. Number two—when was the last time you couldn't hear them coming from a mile away?"

She laughed, then sighed as his fingers worked their magic. "We're supposed to be going over the munchkins' Christmas list."

"It's not going anywhere. Sara?"

She opened her eyes. His were narrowed in concern, only inches away, his breath a warm breeze on her skin.

"Are you afraid Cal's coming after you?" he asked.

Drawing back a little, she sighed. The tension she'd released bunched up again in her shoulders. "Possibly."

"Why?"

Ethan had a right to ask, she knew. After all, she was living in his house. "Ordinarily, a custodial parent can't take the child away, like out of state, unless both parents agree. Right before Thanksgiving we were having a heated argument and he threatened to withhold child support and kick us out of the apartment his parents owned. Then he started taunting me about not being able to give Misty the kind of Christmas she was used to, and I lost my cool and told him we didn't need him or his money and so on…you get the picture.

"Well, he tends to say impulsive things when he's angry and when he told me to go ahead and leave and see how far I could get, I took him at his word. I packed a few things and we left. I knew it would be tough, but it was a lot tougher having to look into Misty's face after she heard her dad screaming at me every week."

"So you figure that when he cooled off and realized you were gone he'd come after you."

She nodded. "Like I said, he doesn't like to lose. But more than that, his parents are probably seeing red. Misty is their first grandchild, and even though they don't give a damn about her most of the time, they'd want to preserve the family image for the holidays."

"Ah." He nodded. "So Cal would want her back before Christmas."

"Yup. I just hope he's chasing his tail in Houston."

"Do your mom and sister know where you are?"

She winced. "Let's not talk about me anymore."

"Okay." He drew her back against him. "Shall we discuss the girls' list?"

She let her head drop to his shoulder, enjoying the warmth and comfort he so freely gave. Volunteering information about himself was a different story. She wanted to know more about Emily, about what kept him grieving for so long. But she was afraid to ask.

"Actually, they aren't being too unreasonable in their requests. If you don't count the chemistry set." And the fact that Misty wants to stay on the ranch forever, but Sara omitted that small detail.

He chuckled and held the list out so they could both see it. "I suppose we can get all of this stuff in Andersonville at one of those new fancy stores they've built."

"First of all, we aren't getting everything on the list. What we need to decide is what we should get."

He reared his head back. "Why can't we get everything?"

She straightened and turned to look at him. "Because not only would it cost a fortune, it isn't good for kids to get everything they ask for."

"Christmas only comes once a year," he muttered in a grumpy voice.

"You were willing to overlook the entire day until I insisted on a tree."

"That was before."

"Before what?"

He sighed. "I thought we were going to talk about the list."

"That's exactly what we're talking about." She frowned. "I know you understand that it isn't good for kids to think they can have anything they want. Life doesn't work that way.''

"I know you're right." He rubbed the side of his jaw. "But I have some making up to do. I didn't always know where they were at Christmas or birthdays. Jenna moved around a lot."

"Guess what?" This time she took his hand. "You couldn't possibly give them more than your presence. They are thrilled to be here spending time with you."

A reluctant smile lifted his lips. "That doesn't mean we can't fill up the bottom of that tree."

She made a sound of exasperation and released his hand. "You're a big kid yourself, know that?"

His smile broadened.

"I can't tell you what to do with your nieces, but Misty is going to have to settle for two presents from Santa and one from me. And a stocking with a few little things in it."

"If it's about the money, I—"

She put a finger to his lips. "Misty is going to have a wonderful Christmas and it will have little to do with how many presents she gets."

His warm breath swirled around her finger, the roughness of stubble grazed her skin and inspired sexy thoughts. Dangerous thoughts. She quickly lowered her hand. "The closer it gets to Christmas the worse shopping will be. Do you think we can go tomorrow?"

"Sure." He had an odd look on his face. Probably because her withdrawal had been so abrupt. "I guess we can ask Erika to keep an eye on the other two.

She's going to be thirteen next month and she's pretty responsible.''

He was right. On the other hand, if anything came up.... ''How long do you think we'll be gone?''

''I'll ask Sam to work near the house. If Erika needs anything, he'll be within hollering distance.''

Relieved, Sara smiled. ''Perfect. What time shall we leave?''

He shrugged. ''Eight? Nine? Erika can help the girls make sandwiches for their lunch,'' he said, and Sara nodded. ''Sam will make sure they get supper.''

She made a face. ''We'll be back long before then.''

''No, we won't.'' He brought her hand back to his mouth and kissed her palm. ''We're eating dinner out. Just the two of us.''

Chapter Twelve

Ethan woke up early and washed his truck. Inside and out. It had been so damn cold that by the time he arrived at the house at nine-thirty to pick up Sara, he still hadn't warmed up.

Only his right boot had made it onto the porch steps when she appeared at the door. Her face looked a little flushed against her light pink sweater, and she wore the same wool skirt she'd had on the last time they'd gone to Andersonville. The one that wouldn't allow her to climb into the truck without his help. His palms immediately began to itch.

"Ready?" he asked unnecessarily, when she clicked the door closed behind her.

"Ready." She smiled as she pulled on her gloves, but she looked nervous.

So was he. It had been a hell of a long time since he'd gone on a date. Not that this was a date, exactly. He would never have asked her to dinner if they weren't already going to town to Christmas shop.

She waited a moment, then edged past him when he forgot to move. He followed her to the passenger side of the truck and opened the door a split second before she placed her gloved hand on the handle.

Her smile of thanks faded as she stared at the high seat. "Oh, no. I shouldn't have worn this skirt. I forgot."

"No problem." He eagerly clasped the sides of her waist and lifted her onto the seat.

Her flush deepened. "Did you talk to Sam?"

"All taken care of." He went around the front and climbed in beside her, and it took no time at all for the cab to feel toasty warm. In fact, things had started heating up the moment he'd touched her.

"Will he look in on them a few times?"

"Yup. And Erika won't even know he's checking on them." When Ethan looked over at her, he saw that she was staring at his new jeans, dark blue, not even washed yet.

He cleared his throat. "Where to first?" he asked before they'd even pulled out of the drive.

"I saw a department store when we went grocery shopping, but I don't know the name of it."

"I know which one you mean." His shirt was new, too, and he stuck his finger between his neck and the collar to loosen it some. "You look nice, Sara."

"Thanks. You do, too."

He mumbled a return thanks, and then they fell into an awkward silence. Finally, he turned on the radio and they listened to Clint Black, Trisha Year-wood and Shania Twain philosophize about life and the opposite sex.

By the time Ethan parked the truck across from the gaudily decorated Andersonville sheriff's department, he was never so glad to see a crowd in his life. A parade of shoppers lined the sidewalks on both sides of the streets, some of the people slowing things down by gawking at display windows and the giant Christmas tree rising from the middle of the town square.

"Good grief! I never would have guessed there would be this many people here." Sara dodged a redheaded young woman with an armful of packages steamrolling her way down the sidewalk. "I didn't think this many people lived in Andersonville."

"They don't." Ethan slipped an arm around her shoulders and steered them toward the corner where they could safely cross the street. "People come from nearly a hundred miles around to shop here. It's the biggest town south of Taos. That's why I figured we'd have to have dinner here. I knew shopping would take a while."

He felt her turn her head sharply to look at him, but he kept his gaze directed the other way. He was such a damn coward he couldn't even meet her eyes. Right about now she was probably wondering if she'd misunderstood him last night, and that dinner out was a convenience, not a date.

When they got to the corner, after mentally preparing himself for the hurt in her eyes, he reluctantly looked at her.

Hurt, nothing. She looked madder than a wet hen. She shook off his arm and glared back. "You big turkey. Take off your shirt and let's see how far that yellow streak goes."

"What?"

"You know exactly what I'm talking about." She

folded her arms across her chest and ignored the interested stares of a pair of older women.

"Sara." He tried to take her arm, to get them someplace more private.

She jerked away, keeping her arms folded. "Why are you changing your tune now?"

"You mean, about dinner?"

"Exactly."

He sighed, glanced around. Most people kept walking. A few stared as they passed.

"Are you ashamed to be seen with me?"

He looked her directly in the eyes. "Of course not."

"What then?"

"You seemed nervous, and I didn't want you to feel any pressure."

She blinked, and her expression wavered for a moment. "Aren't you a little nervous?"

He snorted. "Nervous? I think my underwear's on backwards."

She pressed her lips together when a plump older woman gave Ethan a funny look before lifting her chin and rushing past them. The amusement left Sara's face when she tilted her head back to look at him again. "You're sure it has nothing to do with me?"

The uncertainty in her voice and face got to him. Cal's carping words were messing up her head; Ethan was sure of it. So brave one minute, her bruised spirit undermined her confidence the next. The bastard had broken her, just like he would a wild horse.

Ethan moved closer, and in front of everyone who

cared to watch, slid his arms around her. "Honey, you couldn't do anything wrong if you tried."

Her eyes wide, she stared up at him. He framed her face with his hands and lowered his mouth to hers. She was so startled, her lips remained parted, and he did everything he could not to slip his tongue between them and steal her sweetness.

Instead, he kept the kiss short, then pulled back to smile at her. A couple of people laughed, someone clapped, others gasped in indignation. He didn't give a damn about a single one. All he wanted was to reassure Sara.

She blinked. "If we get arrested, it's your fault."

He chuckled. "I can take the heat. Ready to do some shopping?"

She nodded, and he couldn't be more grateful. Another minute pressed to her soft body and he'd have to buy a bigger pair of jeans.

"You cheated." Sara stared at the mound of packages filling the cab of the truck. "That is way more than your half of the list."

"Just hold on there." Ethan unlocked the door, then relieved her of the three sacks of toys and socks. "Who said that's all for the kids? I have other people to buy for."

She didn't believe him for an instant. Shortly after they'd arrived in town they agreed to split up since they weren't accomplishing much together. But after their conversation last night, she should have known better than to trust he'd stick to his portion of the list. "Like who?"

"Like Sam, for instance."

"Right."

"And Jenna."

Sara gave him a disbelieving look, and then started sifting through the packages from the department store.

"Hey." He snatched one out of her hand. "You can't poke around like that."

"Well, that's silly. Who do you think is going to end up wrapping all this stuff?"

A mysterious smile curved his mouth.

"There had better not be anything in there for me. We agreed not to—"

"I'm hungry. I need some lunch."

"Ethan."

Ignoring her warning tone, he stacked her packages on top of the rest, then locked the door. "There's a little place around the corner that makes the best cheeseburgers this side of Santa Fe. How does that sound?"

"Evasive."

"Come on. They make some fine apple cobbler, too."

She let him take her hand, and they walked side by side, looking in store windows at the Christmas displays and dodging other shoppers. Maybe it was because of the holiday stress or because it was almost that time of the month, but Sara couldn't decide if she wanted to crawl into a ball and weep, or stand in the middle of the town square and scream her head off.

Ethan had her so confused her head literally hurt. A needling pain, right between the eyes, had plagued her most of the morning. Ever since he'd kissed her. Having spent the next hour gritting her teeth wishing for more hadn't helped the problem.

"Here we are." He stopped in front of a small diner that had Bubba's Burgers painted in red on the window, and opened the door. "It's crowded, but there's an empty booth."

She stepped inside first but then let him lead the way. Even for that short distance he took her hand. His touch was really getting to her—and she had gloves on. Boy, she was in sorry shape.

When he stopped at the booth to let her get seated first, she sat near the edge to discourage him from sitting beside her. He made no comment and, in fact, showed no reaction when he slid in across from her.

A pair of well-worn plastic menus were sandwiched between the salt and pepper shakers, and he handed one to her. "It's been a while since I've been here, but I doubt anything's changed."

He glanced briefly at the list of burgers. "There it is. The bacon double cheese with red onion, guacamole and salsa." He was so busy drooling over the description, he didn't see her cringe. "It comes with garlic fries that'll make you a new woman."

"Hmm, I'm sort of just getting used to the current me. I think I'll pass." The sandwiches looked more interesting to her. "I think I'll have the chicken salad Santa Fe style on rye." She looked up to find a strange expression on his face. "What? Bad choice?"

He blinked and shook his head. "Emily always ordered that," he said quietly. "She swore it was the best thing on the menu."

"I'm sorry. I'll have something else."

He blinked again, looking slightly annoyed. "Of course you won't. I only meant that it should be good."

She stared down at the menu. It didn't matter. Her appetite was gone. "We shouldn't have come here."

"Sara, I'm sorry. It's okay. I—I—" He exhaled a muttered curse. "This place is fine. I feel guilty because I hadn't even thought of Emily until you mentioned the chicken salad." He sighed. "I used to think about her all the time, and lately I—" He stared down at his clasped hands. "The memories are starting to fade."

"They haven't faded, Ethan. It's just that you have more going on in your life these days. The girls have soaked up a lot of your time and energy. Plus the excitement of the holidays." He looked so forlorn, her heart ached for him. "You aren't forgetting Emily. You're reacquainting yourself with life."

He looked helplessly into her eyes, and she could tell he wanted to believe her. But fear and guilt were powerful detractors.

"You two decided what you want?" The short gray-haired waitress barely looked at them as her raspy smoker's voice made them jump. She licked the tip of her pencil and poised it above the pad of paper. "We're all out of the specials. You gotta get here earlier for them."

"I bet you tell that to all the cowboys," Ethan said, his mouth beginning to curve in a grin. "Huh, Madge?"

The woman slowly lifted her narrowing gaze from her notepad, then stared at him as if she'd seen a ghost. Then she plucked the menu out of his hand

and hit him on the arm with it. "You ol' son of a gun, where have you been hiding?"

He shrugged. "Been busy. But if I'd remembered how pretty you were, I'd've been in a whole lot sooner."

"Oh, go on." She smacked him with the menu again, then patted her beehive hairdo. "Now you probably expect me to have Hal put extra guacamole on your burger."

Ethan laughed. "Now, how did you remember that?"

Sara was vaguely aware that Madge had turned her attention her way, but she was too busy staring at Ethan. The transformation in him was astounding. He sounded young and carefree. He almost looked different, too. It was the weirdest thing....

"She wants the Santa Fe chicken salad on rye," Sara heard Ethan say, and she snapped out of her preoccupation, blinking rapidly, then staring dumbly at Madge.

"I'm sorry. Were you speaking to me?" she asked, feeling like she'd just stepped through the looking glass.

"That's okay, hon. Ethan here took care of you." The waitress smiled kindly, and then jotted something on her notepad before she left to deliver a check.

"I'm sorry," Sara said. "I guess I spaced out for a minute."

"It's good to see Madge. I've known her since I started coming here in high school." He stared off, fond memories of happier times erasing some of the tension that seemed to hover permanently around his mouth. "If it was late at night, she used to smell our breaths, make sure we hadn't been drinking and then make us promise to call her once we got home."

He shook his head. "She's worn that same hair-style for twenty years. The same glasses, too, I think."

Sara smiled. "You have a nice laugh."

His startled eyes met hers.

"You should do it more often."

Tension resumed its post around his mouth. Something she'd said had obviously upset him. But what? All she'd said was—

"Ethan?" Madge reappeared. "Hal wants to see you but he's got too many burgers on the grill, so he said to get your sorry butt back there in the kitchen."

"You mean no one's put that old buck out to pasture yet?" Ethan asked with a straight face.

"Yeah, you go tell him that. Me, I gotta go take table number five's order before the old fart with the straw hat has a coronary."

Sara chuckled. "She sure is colorful."

"I'm guessing she's about seventy by now, but she sure hasn't slowed down. Mind if I leave you for a moment? I won't be long."

"Of course not. Go."

Ethan wasn't gone but a few seconds when Madge reappeared. Her gaze flicked cautiously toward the kitchen where Ethan had gone, then she said, "I don't know who you are, Miss, but I'm glad to see you brought our boy back among the living.

It ain't right for a body to grieve that long. Not someone like him. He always loved life too much.''

Madge left as quickly as she'd appeared, and Sara stared after her, wondering about the man Ethan had been before his wife had died. She would love to ask Madge some questions, but out of respect for Ethan's privacy she wouldn't.

Sara sighed. Oh, who was she kidding? She'd do it in a heartbeat if she had the opportunity or didn't think she'd get caught. He was just so darn tight-lipped. Last night had been the perfect chance for him to unload. But he obviously wasn't ready.

"Try this."

She looked up as he slid back into the booth and set a tall glass of what looked to be a vanilla shake in front of her. "What is it?"

"Sort of a cross between a malt and a shake. It's Madge's specialty."

He stuck a straw into the middle of the frothy concoction, and the mixture was so thick the straw stayed right there. Sara picked up a spoon and tried a dab.

"Wow! This *is* good." She took another spoonful. A much bigger one this time.

"Uh-uh." Ethan slid it closer to him. "Don't ruin your lunch."

When he slurped up a mouthful, she narrowed her gaze at him. "Why is it okay for you?"

"What?" He looked at her in surprise. "This is nothing. I could finish this off, eat my half-pound burger and fries, and still have another one of these."

"Don't underestimate me."

With a patronizing expression he took another big sip, then used the spoon to scoop up what he couldn't get through the straw.

"Madge?" Sara smiled at the waitress as she stopped by their table. "May I please have one of those?"

The woman's over-plucked eyebrows rose. "Before your sandwich?"

Sara nodded.

Ethan grunted. "No problem. I'll finish what she can't handle."

Sara only smiled. He had no idea....

As it turned out, their food and the malted shake were ready at the same time. Madge carried the tray to the table, so overloaded that she had to set it down in order to transfer the heaping plates.

Ethan's plate wasn't even a plate; it was a platter, filled with so much food you couldn't see a speck of the white ceramic. It was a good thing Sara was hungry. Her mounds of chicken salad resembled the San Juan Mountains.

"This looks great, Madge," Ethan said, then eyed Sara's plate with amusement before he started digging in to his fries.

The older woman sighed happily, then left to clear a nearby table.

Sara carefully arranged her sandwich, stacking the rounds of tomato and the alfalfa sprouts on top, and then cut it in quarters. She nibbled her dill pickle and two fries. She looked over at Ethan. He'd already eaten half his burger.

"You want a bite?" he asked, and when she said yes, his eyes widened. "It's kind of messy."

"No problem." She reached across and cut herself a good-size chunk. It was thick and she had to smash it down a little to fit it into her mouth, but she polished it off, then daintily wiped her mouth with her napkin. "You're right. Yum! I'd have that if we came back here. Although my sandwich is really good, too."

She returned to her own chicken salad, mindful of his incredulous gaze as she slowly but steadily ate every last morsel on her plate. Then she set it aside and slid the shake in front of her. She tried using the straw first.

"It's melted a little and gotten nice and creamy." She took another sip, then made an appreciative sound. "I like it even better like this. Want to try it?"

He gave her a bland look. "Okay, you made your point. Now don't make yourself sick."

Smiling wryly, she stirred the straw around. "I knew you'd think that I was just being stubborn. The truth is, I usually have a very healthy appetite."

His gaze unconsciously lowered to her shoulders, her chest, her arms before his frown of disbelief returned to her face. She was deceptively slim, always had been, but she'd also been a ball of energy from the time she could crawl. Once she'd entered school, she always kept up with the boys in the cafeteria.

She took another sip, and then settled back in the booth. "Cal used to be horrified at how much I ate. It didn't matter that I was active and obviously needed that amount of food because I never gained weight. He didn't say much until after we got married. And then Cal's Commandments were issued."

Ethan stiffened, his brows furrowing to form two deep creases between them.

"That was a joke. Sort of." She shrugged. "I mean, it was something I privately called his petty rules and regulations. But I'll never forget our first dinner at his parents' house as a married couple. We had Cornish game hens and the best roasted potatoes I'd ever had, so when Hazel, their maid, offered me seconds I accepted.

"Cal went nuts. He told her to take the food away, and that from then on I would learn to eat like a lady. I was so humiliated I could barely pick up my water glass."

Ethan's eyes simmered with anger. "Did he ever once lay a hand on you?"

"Never. He didn't have to. One look used to send me cowering. After that night, I tried to reduce my food portions, and then ate half of what I put on my plate. I was starving all the time and losing weight. What I finally ended up doing was hiding food. All over the house, anywhere I didn't think he'd find it. I lived like that for almost eight years." She vehemently shook her head and looked him straight in the eyes. "I won't do it again. I eat what I want, when I want. And I go where I please."

Ethan stared at her a long time without saying anything or giving his thoughts away. It was almost as though the information was too much for him to digest. And then a slow smile curved his lips. "Want me to order you another malted?"

She laughed. "Even I have my limits."

"Guess I'd better order myself one then, because I'm not getting any of that one, am I?"

"Not a chance." The giddiness of freedom and grit made her pleasantly light-headed. She closed her eyes and savored the taste of the creamy malt, and her own determination.

"Well, you two did a mighty fine job here."

Sara opened her eyes to find Madge staring in awe at their clean plates.

"You and Hal are still the best cooks this side of the Rio Grande," Ethan said. "In fact, I aim on sweet-talking you into making me another one of your malts."

Madge's gaze drew to the one in front of Sara. "You plan on finishing that?"

Sara grinned. "Yes, ma'am, I am."

"Boy, you sure aren't like Emily."

The second the words were out of the woman's mouth her face paled. She brought a shaky hand to her ruby-red lips, her eyes full of misery. "I'm sorry, Ethan."

He smiled sadly. "It's okay."

No, it wasn't, Sara suddenly realized with a heavy heart. That was their major stumbling block. She wasn't Emily.

Chapter Thirteen

Ethan wished with all his heart that Madge hadn't brought up Emily earlier today. He knew it had been an honest slip of the tongue, and poor Madge was probably still beating herself over the head because of it, but what disturbed him most was Sara's reaction.

He passed her one package after another and watched her pile them in the middle of the truck's cab—between their two seats. She'd been quiet ever since lunch, even when they'd shopped together for Erika in one of those new age stores with all the weird gadgets and kooky crystal jewelry. Not even when he pretended to want a fake nose ring like Erika's did he get much of a reaction out of Sara. She just looked at him like he was nuts, and then moved to the counter to pay for some earrings.

Maybe she was irritated with him for kissing her earlier on the street corner? Nah, she'd been fine up until lunch.

Or maybe she regretted telling him the story about Cal and how he'd tried to control her eating? Just the memory of her expression as she'd replayed her first dinner with Cal's parents made Ethan boiling mad. He'd love to smash the guy right in the face.

She finished stowing their purchases and started to climb up into the truck on her own. He promptly bracketed her waist and helped her in. She was so tiny it was pretty amazing how much food she could pack away.

Emily'd been tall, not slim, not fat, just right, but she never ate much. Except she sure had liked chocolate. She'd give up an entire meal just to have a candy bar.

He frowned as he headed for the driver's seat. Had Emily had her secrets, too? Had she ever hidden something from him out of fear he would disagree? Jenna had always accused him of being bullheaded, of needing to have his way. Maybe Emily went along with him to keep the peace.

Disgusted by the direction of his thoughts, he pulled out of the parking place too abruptly, causing the tires to squeal, and netting him several dirty looks. Including one from Sara.

Great. At least he'd finally gotten a reaction out of her.

After traveling in silence for the next ten minutes, she asked, "Weren't we supposed to take that last fork going west?"

"If we were going home we would have."

"Isn't that where we're going?"

"I promised you dinner out."

With something between a laugh and a groan she asked, "How can you think about dinner after what you ate for lunch?"

"That was hours ago." He turned his attention to

her for an instant. The way the setting sun caught her hair gave her a golden-pinkish glow. She looked as though she should be on the glossy cover of a magazine, not sitting in his old truck. He went back to watching the road and trying to rein in his galloping hormones. "Anyway, I figured it's gotta be your feeding time about now."

"Very funny." She sniffed. "Why don't we just pick up a pizza and surprise the girls?"

"Is that what you want to do?"

She didn't answer, and he slid her a questioning look, but she'd sunk back, and his view of her was obstructed by the mountain of packages.

He pulled the truck over onto the shoulder and let it idle a safe enough distance from traffic.

She sat forward. "What are you doing?"

"Is that what you want, Sara?" he asked, turning to her, his wrist draped over the wheel, his hand dangling in a deceptively calm manner.

She moistened her lips. "You mean, pizza?"

"Would you rather have dinner with the girls than spend time alone with me?"

"What are you asking for, Ethan? Dinner? Or something more?"

That was another way she wasn't like Emily. Sara didn't hesitate to speak her mind. He blew out a huff of frustrated air. "I don't know."

She turned and, with a stubborn lift of her chin, stared out the windshield.

"Okay, it's more than dinner."

She blinked, but other than that, she wouldn't cut him any slack.

"I want—" He rolled a shoulder. "The thing is—

All right, dammit, let's just go home.'' He released the brake.

"Coward.''

"What did you say?''

"You heard me.'' She angled her body away and looked out her side window.

"I heard it. I just don't believe you had the nerve to say it.''

She stiffened her back but kept her face averted.

"You stack all these packages between us like you think I might grab you or something, and then—''

Her gaze flew to his. "I did not! Where else were they supposed to go?''

"I offered to put them in the chest in the back. That's where I stow groceries when I go shopping.''

"I didn't know that.'' She started to turn away.

He reached over and caught her chin, forcing her to face him again. "Are you angry because I kissed you today?''

She gave her head a tiny shake. "No,'' she whispered.

"Good. Because I'm going to do it again.'' He leaned toward her, and she readily pushed forward until their lips met, briefly, awkwardly. The packages were like a barricade.

He tried again, this time cupping her nape with his hand, but the kiss ended up more frustrating than satisfying. And to add insult, a carload of teenagers drove by, making catcalls and honking their horn at them.

"Okay, we're out of here.'' He settled back in his

seat, and put the truck into gear. "But we're not going home."

FIFTEEN MINUTES LATER, Sara's heart skipped more than one beat when Ethan pulled into the parking lot of a motel. When she realized he intended to go to the adjoining Italian restaurant, she wasn't sure if she was disappointed or relieved.

It was almost dark, and she thought about convincing him to go home and make sure the girls were all right. But he'd already assured her Sam was taking care of them, and besides, Sara was too excited to call it quits for the evening.

A week ago, the mention of Emily would have thrown Ethan into such a funk he probably would have headed straight home from lunch. Sara didn't fool herself. She knew he had a long way to go before he could actually let go, but this was definitely a start.

It also occurred to her that Ethan's need might be purely physical. In his grief, he'd probably shunned women in all ways. And now, with a carrot dangling so close to his nose, what red-blooded man wouldn't be tempted to nibble?

The thought should have depressed her, except that deep down she knew better. Ethan had more principle than to use someone for his own gratification. Unlike Cal, who'd used her without a qualm: making her feel small so he could feel big, cutting her down inch by inch. Too bad it had taken her so long to figure it out, but at least she'd finally fitted the sad pieces together.

Ethan opened her door and helped her down. "I

guess I should have asked you if you like Italian.'' He didn't release her, but looked down at her with hungry eyes. Goose bumps surfaced her skin. ''Not that we have much choice. This is the only highway back to the Double S and the only restaurant on it. Of course, we could overshoot the ranch and go have Mexican.''

''Italian is fine.'' She wished the streetlight wasn't shining in her face, revealing to him the excitement and longing she wasn't skilled enough to hide.

''Good.'' He tilted her chin up and brushed his lips against hers. It could barely be classified as a kiss, and it annoyed her when he pulled back and took her hand.

After they'd walked several feet, she said, ''Wait a minute.''

He stopped, gave her a bewildered look, and nearly stumbled when she reached an arm around his neck, hauled him down to her level and laid a kiss on him that would leave a buzz in his ears for days.

She teased his surprised lips open, pushed her tongue inside enough to taunt him and make the muscles at the back of his neck bunch and tighten. Then she let go and lowered herself until her feet were flat again, and took a deep breath. ''Okay, now we can go.''

He didn't move, only stared as though he wasn't sure what had just happened.

Her heart pounded like crazy at her boldness, but she managed to walk without tripping or landing on her rear end. By the time she arrived at the restaurant, he was beside her, pushing the door open. She thanked him politely, certain her chin was quivering, then stepped inside and waited for the hostess to approach them.

Fortunately, the woman addressed Ethan. Sara wasn't certain she could speak…coherently, at least. It wasn't just the kiss or her audacity that had her in need of a respirator, but they were parked at a motel, for crying out loud. Where were her thoughts *supposed* to go? He couldn't be that dense.

She cast a sideways glance at him slipping off his jacket while talking to the hostess. That he seemed so composed further irritated Sara. Until she realized why he'd had to remove his jacket—and drape it in front of himself.

The heat climbed Sara's face as she followed the hostess to a table in the non-smoking section, which turned out to be a secluded booth in the corner. Only two other couples were in the dining room, seated up front, closer to the door, and a man sat by himself at the bar.

Sara quickly slid in first and tried not to look at the front of Ethan's jeans as he sat beside her. When the hostess asked if she could take his jacket, he politely refused and left it on his lap.

"Nice place," Sara said casually as soon as the hostess left. "Do you come here often?"

"Once, years ago. This was Jenna's hangout. I hope all these empty tables don't mean the place has slid downhill since then."

"It is a weeknight, and not exactly the dinner hour."

"True." He looked around the room, lingering on

the Chianti bottle display as if it held some fascination, and she realized he was as nervous as she was.

"You like wine?" she couldn't resist asking.

"Nope. I'm a beer-drinker myself. And that's generally only in the summer."

"Oh." Now, she was looking idly around the dimly lit room.

"This is—"

"Let's—"

They both spoke at once. Ethan backed off first. "You go ahead," he said.

She sighed. "Do you realize we're acting like two schoolkids on their first date?"

"Yup."

"And?"

He frowned and shifted away as if he thought she was going to bite him. "And what?"

"And don't you have anything to say about that?"

He shrugged, looking so adorably confused she didn't know if she wanted to smack him or kiss him again.

The waiter appeared with a list of the specials, and Sara tried her darndest to listen, but it was hopeless. When he was finished, she ended up ordering the standard spaghetti and meatballs and a glass of red wine.

Ethan gave his order, and, after the waiter disappeared, she waited for Ethan to resume their conversation. But he avoided her gaze and used the handle of his fork to make invisible patterns on the red-and-white-checked tablecloth.

"Ethan?"

"I know, I know." He flexed his shoulder. "I'm just trying to figure out what to say here."

A smile tugged at her mouth. "I don't want things to be awkward between us because we don't have the children around to run interference."

"The children have nothing to do with it."

She stared at his somber profile. "Then why are we acting this way?"

He looked at her, his face both wonderfully and frighteningly close. "This is between us, Sara. Even with the kids around I know you've got to feel it, too."

She nodded. "Yeah, that's what I mean. With the kids under foot we have a distraction. Plus, we can't very well—" She shrugged, and feeling shy all of a sudden, lowered her gaze to stare at his plaid flannel collar. "You know…"

He let the silence go on for so long she started getting fidgety, and then he lifted her chin. "You mean this?"

His gaze held hers captive as his mouth inched toward hers, and she automatically strained up to meet him. Their lips touched lightly, and then he angled his head and dove in deep.

She didn't resist. No one was around, and even if they had been she didn't think she could refuse him. He was right. Too much had been simmering and sizzling between them. Warmth spread throughout her body like flowing lava, and when she laid her hand on his thigh, the tips of her fingers brushed the hardness growing beneath his jacket.

It was a good thing they were in a public place,

that they were forced to restrain themselves, or she wasn't sure what would happen. She could almost imagine his hands on her breasts, his mouth, his tongue...

She sensed a movement at the table and drew back a little. Ethan did, too, after pressing one last long, hard kiss on her mouth, and they both looked at the basket of bread and two glasses of water that hadn't been on the table a moment ago.

"Well, that's embarrassing," Sara murmured, and attempted to straighten her hair.

"Ah, hell, we're probably making their day."

Ethan covered her mouth with his again before she could utter a syllable of protest. When he ran his tongue along the inside of her lower lip, objecting was the last thing on her mind.

Under the protection of the tablecloth, she slid her hand farther beneath his jacket and cupped his hardness through the denim.

His breath caught and his tongue stilled. He withdrew. Ever so slightly. Just enough to whisper, "You can't do that, Sara. You can't..."

But he didn't try to stop her, and her hand flexed over him, mostly from nervous excitement at her boldness, the hungry desire swelling in her chest. Sexually, Cal had been the only man in her life, and after her experience with him she'd never thought she'd ever crave anyone physically again. But that was before she'd met Ethan. Even his woodsy scent fueled her new addiction.

He'd grown incredibly hard and big, and with a soft groan he finally moved her hand away. She understood. She was so hot and wet that she didn't think she could get up right now and be able to walk normally.

Slowly, he left her mouth and his lips brushed a trail up her jaw to her ear. "You make me crazy," he whispered, his warm breath sending small shock waves to her nerve endings.

"I don't mean to," she whispered back, unable to open her eyes. "I just want…"

"What, Sara?" His tongue traced the shell of her ear. "Tell me what you want."

Her eyes fluttered open. No one was in sight. They'd probably scared everyone away. "I, uh…" She swallowed. "I want to stop starting things we can't finish."

He pulled back to look at her. His eyes were so hooded, she couldn't read them. He lifted his hand to her face and let his fingers trail her jaw as if he were compelled to touch her. "Can't or won't?"

She blinked, uncertain of his meaning.

He kissed the side of her neck, the skin below her ear. "Are we going to finish this, Sara?"

Her breath caught. She'd accused him of being a coward before. Now wasn't the time for her new-found bravado to fail her. "Yes."

"Tonight?"

She nodded jerkily. "We could go next door."

His breath rushed over her skin; ragged and warm, it felt like satin sheets and sex. And then he muttered a curse.

Startled, she jerked back. And saw why he'd reacted. The waiter approached with a tray of food.

"Here are your salads," he said, setting the

chilled plates before them, a smug grin lurking at the corners of his mustache.

Ethan groaned to himself. He was tempted to tell the guy to keep the salads and the entrées and give him the check instead, but from the look on Sara's face he figured that would only further embarrass her.

"Would you like fresh ground pepper with that?" the young man asked.

Sara shook her head.

Ethan mumbled, "No thanks."

"How about some freshly grated parmesan cheese?"

The look Ethan gave the man sent him scurrying back to the kitchen without another word.

Sara picked up her fork. It shook slightly. "This looks good. It's hard to find nice cherry tomatoes this time of year."

He sighed. "You've changed your mind."

"About next door?" She shook her head.

"You can. I'll understand."

She gave him a tiny smile. "I know. But I want to make love to you," she said softly.

Ethan ate his salad in record time. When his lasagna arrived, he took three bites, then laid his utensils aside. Sara ate more slowly but left most of her meal. She did polish off her wine, though.

The waiter seemed confused when he returned to check on them and saw how much food they'd left, and Ethan told him to bring the bill. When the young man asked if they'd like dessert, they both snapped "no" at the same time.

"I'm never coming back here again," Sara whispered on their way out the door. "Lord, but they must be having a time laughing in the kitchen."

He chuckled. "I don't suppose I'll be coming back any time soon either. Here. Put this around your shoulders."

He offered her his jacket, but she shook her head. He didn't blame her. The cold air felt good. Every time his thoughts strayed to what lay ahead, he felt all warm and flushed.

"I'll go check into a room. You can wait in the truck, if you like," he said.

"I'd like to call the girls. You know, just make sure everything is all right."

Ethan dug into his pocket for change and squinted at the lighted area under the red flashing Vacancy sign. "There's a pay phone over there near the office door. We're only about an hour from home so if there's any reason to head back, it won't take long."

She met his gaze, and then hers flitted away.

He guided them toward the office, wondering if she knew he was offering her a graceful way out. She could use the call to say the kids needed them, and they'd skip the motel. He hoped she didn't. He hoped she wanted him as much as he wanted her.

She stopped a few feet away from the phone and cleared her throat. "How much longer shall I tell them we'll be?"

"I'll leave that one up to you, Sara." He leaned down and kissed her gently on the lips. "After I check us in, I'll call Sam."

She gave a quick nod, and ran a palm up and down her opposite arm. Without asking, he slipped the jacket over her shoulders, then pressed some coins into her free hand.

He smiled. "I'll be right back."

"Ethan?"

He'd already turned to push through the door, but he stopped, and she took a step toward him.

She cleared her throat again. "It's been sort of a long time for me, and…" She visibly swallowed. "I just hope you aren't expecting—"

"Sara…" Ethan wanted to laugh. It had been so long for him he was damn glad one part of him still knew what to do. He sighed, and hugged her briefly to him. "We're in the same boat. How about we agree to no expectations?"

She nodded against his chest and gave him a squeeze around his middle, and then stepped back with a sweet shy smile curving her mouth. "Deal."

"I'll be right back."

"I'm counting on it."

He gave her a long smoldering look, then headed inside the office.

Chapter Fourteen

The room's color scheme was blue. The carpet was a grayish-blue, the drapes a blur of blue and lavender tulips, and the queen-size quilt had wide navy and taupe stripes. The combination was in no way appealing, but then again, Sara was too nervous to give it a second thought.

"Not exactly the Ritz, is it?" Ethan frowned at the two cigarette burns on the blue vinyl chair near the window. He brought his gaze back to her. "We don't have to stay here."

"I know." She dropped her purse on the bed. "It's fine. Really." She tried to give him a reassuring smile, and hoped she didn't look as nervous as she felt.

He kept his gaze on her while he removed his Stetson and tossed it on the dresser. The only time he'd had it off all day was at lunch and dinner and it had left a ridge in his hair.

Sara took the four steps necessary to reach him and raked her fingers through the indention, lifting the soft wavy strands that pressed to his scalp.

Smiling down at her, Ethan put his hands on either side of her waist. "I've been wearing hats so long I think the ridge is permanent."

"So, do you sleep with your hat on, too, cowboy?"

His gaze held hers steady. "You want to find out?"

Her heart slammed against the wall of her chest and her fingers began to massage his scalp. The added pressure encouraged him to lower his head and his lips claimed hers in a knee-weakening kiss.

When he slid his hands under her sweater and up her back, she melted against him, until her breasts ached with the feel of his hard chest. She slid her hands down to his shirt and started unfastening the buttons. His fingers moved down her spine until he reached the clasp of her bra. It suddenly gave way.

She almost gasped in surprise...misgiving... excitement. She abandoned the two remaining buttons and pressed her hands against his naked chest. Soft springy hair brushed her palms, and she smiled. Often she'd wondered if his chest would be smooth or not. She liked the feel of it just the way it was.

His hands moved over her back, spanning her waist, traveling up to massage the muscle between her shoulder blades. When he started to work his way toward her breasts, she stiffened a little. Cal had always said they were too small. What would Ethan think?

He must have sensed her anxiety or felt her body tighten because his exploration immediately stopped. "Having second thoughts, honey?" he asked softly. "If you are, it's okay."

She shook her head and concentrated on unfastening his last two buttons. After pushing his shirt aside, she stared at his chest. It was firm with brown nipples, not too much hair, and he had a taut stomach with some subtle definition. He was truly beautiful in her eyes. The thought of him seeing her naked made her even more nervous.

This wasn't Cal, she sternly reminded herself. Ethan wasn't anything like her ex-husband. In fact, Ethan was everything Cal wasn't. Was that the attraction? The infatuation? Was she being a total fool? Of course, everyone had their faults. Ethan was no exception.

It didn't matter, really. Tonight would not launch a relationship. She knew that. In a week or so she'd be gone. The thought hurt like a hundred pinpricks. That's where being foolish came in—to harbor any hope that tonight would end up anything more than, hopefully, great sex with someone she liked and respected.

And if she continued to imagine how it would feel to be loved completely by someone as loyal and kind and dedicated as Ethan Slade, she *would* be a total fool.

"Sara, talk to me." Ethan forced her chin up. "Something's wrong."

"No." She shook her head. "Not with us. Old baggage, you know?"

"I know," he said, closing his eyes and pulling her close. "I know."

She enjoyed the warm, safe feeling of his arms banded around her, of her cheek pressed against his soft chest hair, and it felt so right her apprehension dissolved. She rubbed her palm up his chest and felt his nipple bead beneath it. Without hesitation, she stuck out her tongue and touched the tip to his nipple.

His shudder encouraged her to take the nub between her lips, to bite lightly, to lick away any sting. He groaned, his breath quickening. The swell beneath his jeans pressed against her belly.

"Sara." He held her away from him, took a deep breath, his chest rising and falling as he stared at her with unfocused eyes. "Don't, Sara."

She was about to move in and capture his other nipple when he tugged the hem of her sweater up. Automatically she raised her arms, and he pulled the sweater over her head and flung it on the bed. With impatience in his hands and eyes, he slipped the bra straps off her shoulders and let it all slide to the floor. The worshipful expression on his face made her breath catch.

"You're so beautiful, Sara." His gaze lifted to her face. "You're incredible."

She believed him. The truth was in his eyes. It boosted her confidence. "Take your shirt off," she ordered, barely recognizing her own voice.

He quickly did as she asked, and she stared, spellbound by his magnificence. It wasn't that he had the perfect body...far from it. He had a number of small scars near his right shoulder and a long faded one at his waist, a peculiar looking birthmark by his navel. But the small imperfections all added to his character. He worked hard, he loved the land and it showed.

On tiptoes, she reached up and kissed the web of scars on his shoulder.

"Barbed wire," he said with a grimace. "Just jumped out and bit me."

His humor disarmed her, and when he cupped a breast she jumped a little. He started to withdraw, but she forced his hand back to her breast, to the nipple that had already pearled. His gaze bore into her for a moment, and then he lowered his head and drew the puckered flesh into his mouth.

She moaned at the sheer pleasure of his tongue on her sensitive skin. Her only regret was that they weren't horizontal, because her knees were becoming incredibly useless. The greedy way he suckled her just about sent her over the edge.

Even though she clung to his shoulders, she felt her body slipping, and in the next second she sank to the edge of the bed. Ethan followed her down, crawling up her body to suckle her other breast as she lay back.

She hated that she still had her skirt on. She wished she could just make it disappear. She wished Ethan was bare, too, and that his body could seep into hers. It was odd to feel so sexual, almost scary, but powerful, too.

Ethan moved up to kiss her. He started out gently, but his mouth started making more and more demands as his hand slid up the outside of her thigh. "Let's get the rest of these clothes off," he whispered hoarsely, already searching for her zipper.

She instantly found his belt buckle and released it. His snap and zipper weren't quite as easy. He was so hard, his jeans were exceptionally tight, and she feared doing damage. Her hesitation and thoughtful probing seemed to inflame him and he groaned her name.

He unzipped her, had trouble with the clasp, and in apparent impatience, reached under her skirt again. This time he stroked up her inner thigh and slid a finger under her panties. He found her wetness, and, with another groan, his mouth came down on hers again.

She fumbled some more with his zipper, desperate to feel him, but suddenly he stopped kissing her and muttered a curse.

She gasped and withdrew her hand. "I hurt you."

His breathing was ragged. "No. No, you didn't." He kissed her briefly. "I forgot something."

"You—" She shook away the fog. "What?"

"Condoms. I forgot to get condoms."

It took a few seconds for the problem to sink in, and then she winced. "I feel so foolish. I forgot, too."

He rolled onto his side and propped his head up with his hand. With his other one, he trailed a path between her breasts, his gaze following the motion. "I think I know where I can buy them."

"Where?"

"That gas station we passed a few miles back."

She whimpered when he lightly pinched a nipple. "They sell those things at gas stations?"

He stopped. "They have one of those mini-marts inside. Don't you think they'd sell them there?"

"I have no idea." She wished he'd caress her breasts again. She shifted to give him the hint.

"It's been so long since I've used one." He

sighed, his gaze drifting down to her chest. "I don't know. I'll have to try."

The longing on his face sent a flush over her entire body. "You'd better hurry."

"Uh-huh." He leaned closer and kissed her thoroughly.

She finally pulled back. "I seriously think you should go now."

"Trying to get rid of me?" He nipped her earlobe.

"Yes." She cupped him over the denim and applied some pressure. "The place may close, and..."

Groaning, he gently pulled her hand away. "This is not the way to get me out the door."

She laughed softly. "Maybe I should go with you. Who knows what might happen on the way back?"

A sexy smile curved his mouth, and he started to roll towards her. "There are other things we could do that—"

"Hey." She edged back. Dare she ask what he had in mind? Two ideas flitted through her head. They gave her a serious jolt of heat. "We're wasting time."

He sighed and flopped on his back to stare at the ceiling for a second, and then he bolted up. "You're right."

She watched him struggle into his shirt, her gaze constantly wandering back to his straining fly. Waiting was going to be sheer torture.

"Any particular kind you want?" He grinned when her eyes widened.

"I haven't even seen one before," she admitted.

He looked surprised, and then a mischievous glint

entered his eyes. "Then maybe we should introduce you to the French tickler."

Sara laughed and shuddered at the same time. "That sounds—ominous. Is there really one called that?"

He scooped his truck keys off the dresser, then continued to button his shirt as he went to the door. "Don't worry. We'll be lucky to get the garden variety." He opened the door, then paused. "Lock this after me."

She nodded, and, smiling, she got up as soon as the door closed. It automatically locked, and she doubted it was necessary to use the deadbolt around here, but it gave her a nice feeling to know he was concerned about her. Ignoring her bra, she pulled her sweater over her head and slid the deadbolt home.

As much as she hated the interruption, she decided it was reassuring to know she had no desire to back out of this intimacy with Ethan. Right now, at this particular point in her life, she wanted and needed him. And unless she was gravely mistaken, the same was true for him.

She'd never much believed in fate before, but she did now. This felt too right, too natural to have not been predestined. Feeling like a giddy schoolgirl, she hurried to the window to watch him get into his truck.

At first all she could see was the truck. Ethan was nowhere in sight. She pressed her forehead against the glass to see as far down the sidewalk as she could, but still she didn't see him. That was strange....

She forced the window open, and although it would only slide out a few inches, it was enough for her to get a partial view. Enough for her to spot him. Near the office. In the arms of a blonde.

"I CAN'T believe it." Ethan stepped back to get another look at her. "I can't believe you're here. You look great."

"No, I don't. I've been driving for eleven hours and I look like hell."

He smiled and opened his arms out to her again. "Come here."

She gave him a big hug and laid her head against his chest for a minute. "It's so good to be home."

"You're not there yet. What made you stop here?" They broke apart again.

"I was starting to nod off, and I knew this was the last stop before the Double S where I could get some rest or a few cups of caffeine. Tell me how the girls are doing."

"Fine." Ethan looked into his sister's tired face and his chest ached. Six years had been too long. "I have a woman looking after them. They have a tree and it's all decorated and everything. They're terrific kids—you've done a great job with them, Jenna."

"I had a good teacher." A weary smile curved her pale lips. "We have a lot to talk about."

He glanced at her ringless finger. "No wedding?"

"Nope. I woke up just in time. The guy wasn't right for me. He wouldn't have made a good father for the girls." Shuddering, she crossed her arms and hugged herself. "I must be finally growing up. Scary, isn't it?"

"Downright horrifying."

She lightly punched his arm. "Thanks." And then she frowned. "What are you doing here, anyway?"

He flexed a shoulder, shrugged it. "I was doing some Christmas shopping for the girls and remembered this restaurant you used to talk about, and figured..." he shrugged again, "...why not?"

Her eyebrows rose in disbelief. "I didn't know you liked Italian food. Or Christmas shopping."

He shrugged again, and tried to take an inconspicuous look over his shoulder. Sara couldn't see him from the room, not at this angle, but if she happened to look out and see the truck was still here....

"What's wrong?" Jenna asked. "Don't tell me you have a woman stashed away in one of those rooms?"

Her teasing grin raked dread down his spine. For his part, he didn't care if Jenna knew about Sara. But he figured Sara would have a very different opinion. "Three of them."

She laughed. "Yeah, right."

"Did you just get here?"

"Just now. I thought I'd grab some coffee and then decide what to do. I was going to call you in a minute to warn you I was coming, then possibly spend the night here." She yawned. "Wow, I thought I could drive straight through, but I'm exhausted."

Damn. He couldn't let her drive tonight, and she probably expected him to offer to take her and worry about her car tomorrow. That would be awkward.

He stalled for a minute. "Well, let's see—"

"Let's get one thing straight right now. I'm not asking you to solve my problem. I'm old enough to do that myself. And no, I am not going back with you and leaving my car here. Everything I own, or at least that's important to me, is in that van and I'm not leaving it."

"Okay," he said slowly. "What do you want to do?"

Jenna sighed. "As much as I hate to spend the money, I think I'll check into a room and get a few hours' sleep. I know my daughters. They'll keep me up all night jabbering about every detail of the last nine days."

Ethan had already reached into his pocket. "I'll pay for your room."

"You will not." Her steely gaze met his. "Stop fathering me, Ethan. I'm an adult."

"This has nothing to do with—"

"Ethan!"

He held up his hands in surrender. "Okay."

"Are you headed home now?"

Sighing to himself, he nodded.

Jenna glanced at her wristwatch and made a face. "I'm wondering if you should tell the girls I'm coming. It'll be late and they won't get to sleep."

"Let's surprise them tomorrow morning. That way you can take your time if you feel you need more sleep before you get behind the wheel again."

"You're right. And then I can crash as soon as I get there instead of having to answer a hundred questions." She plowed a hand through her long tangled hair, blonder now than it was when she was young.

He smiled. "I can't call you squirt anymore. That's Denise's name now."

Jenna rolled her eyes. "You can't call me that anyway. I'm almost as tall as you are."

"Right."

She chuckled. "Thanks, Ethan."

"For what?"

She shrugged. "For not arguing with me. For acknowledging I'm an adult and can make my own decisions."

Their shouting arguments flashed through his mind, the nights he stayed up worrying, the day she told him she would never come back. He wanted to ask how long she planned to stay. "I'm glad you're home, Jenna. I've missed you."

Her eyes got bright, and she blinked quickly. "I've missed you, too."

He cleared his throat. "Now, go get some shut-eye."

"Don't start ordering me around," she said, and then her lips curved in a grin. "You'll be glad to know I've been paid back for all the grief I gave you."

"Denise?"

She laughed heartily as she started to back away. "She's just like me, isn't she?"

"Maybe worse."

"Oh, great." She laughed again. "I'll see you in a few hours. Want me to call before I leave?"

He smiled. She *had* grown up. "Thanks."

With a knowing smile, she turned and headed into the motel office.

Ethan waited until he was sure she was busy with the clerk before he hurried back to Sara. He used the key, then knocked when he realized the deadbolt was locked.

The minute she opened the door he knew something was wrong. Her face was pale, and she had trouble meeting his gaze. Her purse was already slung over her shoulder.

"May I come in?" he asked when she hadn't moved.

She didn't respond at first, just looked at him with uncertainty. Had she changed her mind? Had he taken so long that she thought he'd changed his?

"Sure," she said finally, and backed up a step. Her gaze lowered to his empty hands. "Did you make it to the store?"

He shook his head. "We have a slight problem."

"No, we don't." She lifted her chin. "We were being rash. It's not a good idea to jeopardize our relationship. It would make it uncomfortable for the children."

Ethan's gut coiled into a knot. It had taken a lot out of him to put himself out there, to risk her rejection, to shove aside his guilt. "Twenty minutes ago you weren't thinking about the kids."

She glared at him. "Twenty minutes ago I—" She shook her head, misery clouding her face. "Can we just go home, please?"

He didn't understand what was happening. There was a sharp edge to her voice he'd never heard. He'd thought he knew Sara. Enough to believe what she'd wanted was to make love and not just to have sex. But you didn't turn something like that on and off so easily.

"Yeah, we'll go home." He threw the keys on the dresser and rubbed his eyes. "But not for a few more minutes. My sister is in the office checking in."

Chapter Fifteen

"Hey, where are all the packages?" Denise had run out of the house in her stockinged feet to greet them halfway up the sidewalk.

"Why aren't you in bed?" Sara asked a little more sternly than she'd intended.

Unfazed, Denise scowled. "I thought you guys went Christmas shopping. I don't see any bags."

"We did, and we have them." Sara took her by the shoulders and turned her around toward the front door. "Now, would you please go in the house? It's freezing out here."

"But—"

"Denise." Ethan's voice was even sterner, and Denise immediately closed her mouth. "Do as you're told."

She mumbled under her breath all the way up the porch steps and into the house.

"I think we should leave the presents locked in your truck." Sara had barely said a word on the ride back. She'd been too busy mentally kicking herself. "Or maybe you can take them to your place."

They stopped on the porch. The light illuminated

his face, and she could tell he was still upset with her. She should have told him she'd seen him and Jenna, and that she'd harbored the false impression, but she felt like such a silly, jealous fool.

She couldn't imagine how he'd react if he knew the truth. He'd be scared off, she knew for certain. He'd regard her as a clinging vine intent on choking out his freedom, trying to smother his memories of Emily.

"You think they'd peek?" Ethan asked.

"Peek?" She frowned, confused, then remembered their conversation. "Of course they'll peek, given the opportunity."

"Yeah, I guess so." Sighing, he closed his eyes and stretched his neck from side to side. "Let's leave them in the truck."

"Just until tomorrow afternoon. I'll wrap them after lunch, and then we can put them under the tree."

"Not the ones from Santa."

At his appalled look, she smiled. "No, I even have special paper for those presents. I'll leave it all in the truck, if you don't mind."

"Of course not."

"Ethan?"

Their eyes met. His were disturbingly noncommittal. But she knew he was angry, probably even a little hurt. She should explain why she'd behaved as she had earlier. What was worse? To have him think she was fickle, maybe even a tease? Or to let him feel threatened?

He stood looking expectantly at her, not so much as giving away a morsel of his thoughts. There'd been no ugly words. He'd been totally civil, but she just couldn't do it. She'd learned years ago to avoid confrontation.

"I, um, just wanted to say—" She tucked a strand of hair behind her ear. "That, um, I'll wrap your presents if you want."

"Thanks."

"Are you going to tell the girls about Jenna tonight?"

"No, they'll get too excited and won't sleep."

"You're right." God, Sara wished he'd look the least bit interested in talking to her. "You must be excited, too."

"Yeah, it's been a long time."

"Well, it's cold. We should go inside."

He didn't say anything. He just opened the door for her.

With a heavy heart, she led the way inside, blinking, hoping there'd be no sudden ambush of tears. She should have been in his arms right now, both of them naked, sated, comforted. She absolutely couldn't think about that, or she'd lose it.

"Hi, Mom." Misty ran to give her a hug. "Denise said you didn't buy any Christmas presents."

"Don't listen to her." Erika sat sideways in the recliner, her legs hanging over the arm of the chair. "You don't expect them to show you what they bought, do you?"

"Be quiet. No one's talking to you." Denise took Misty's hand and led her toward the hall.

"You're going to bed, I hope," Sara called after them.

"Denise is going to think up ways to find the

packages.'' Erika hopped up. ''By the way, where are they?''

Sara gave her a wry look. ''Nice try.''

The girl grinned. ''I can help you wrap the kids' stuff.''

''I'll think about it.'' Sara's gaze furtively tracked Ethan to the kitchen. Other than saying hi, he'd said nothing to the girls. Of course they were busy jabbering about their presents.

''What's wrong with him?'' Her voice anxious, Erika frowned at his retreating back.

''I don't think shopping is his thing.''

''Oh, yeah. Especially if it was crowded.'' Erika seemed relieved, and a spark of irritation ignited in Sara.

She stared after Ethan and realized what had upset her. For years her emotional state had depended on Cal's moods. When they got up in the morning, she practically asked him how *they* felt. She was probably overreacting with Erika, but she hated to see the girl relieved just because she could explain her uncle's moodiness. It bothered Sara to see any woman's mood depend on a man.

''Anything I need to know about since I called?'' Sara asked, and Erika shook her head. ''Thanks. I appreciate you looking after them.''

Erika yawned and stretched. ''No problem. I love bossing Denise around.''

Sara smiled. ''How about going to bed? I know it's still early for you, but something tells me we're going to have a big day tomorrow.''

''Why?''

Wrong thing to say. Sara knew better. Darn it.

"Lots of cleaning to do before we finish decorating."

Erika's expression fell. "Oh, that." She sighed. "I guess I'll go listen to some music for a while."

As soon as the girl was gone, Sara hurried to the kitchen. She didn't want Ethan leaving before they talked. At least about Jenna, and how he wanted to handle things.

He was staring out the back window, drinking something out of a small glass, so preoccupied he didn't hear her enter. Or at least he didn't turn around.

"Ethan?"

He slowly swung a glance her way.

"We have to talk about tomorrow. About when—" she glanced over her shoulder to make sure they weren't being overheard, and then moved closer to him, "...when your sister comes. I have to prepare a room for her and..."

He leaned closer, and her breath caught when she felt his dance across her cheek. Her gaze fell on the fullness of his lower lip and her pulse picked up speed. What was he doing?

"I couldn't hear you," he said, his expression still maddeningly blank.

"Oh. I didn't want the girls to hear." She swallowed her disappointment. "Which room would you like me to prepare for Jenna?" She thought she saw disappointment in his eyes and her pulse leaped again. "The master bedroom is—"

"No. That stays the way it is."

"Okay. How about the one next to Erika?"

"Fine."

"What did you tell her about me?"

Ethan narrowed his gaze. "What do you mean?"

Sara shrugged. "I assume she knows I'm watching the girls. I just didn't know what else you might have said."

He looked stunned. "She doesn't know you were with me at the motel tonight."

His reaction was like a sharp jab to the ribs. Was he ashamed of her?

"I told her you were the housekeeper, and that you're taking care of the kids."

"Of course." She had to leave. Get to her room. Fast. The back of her eyes burned, and she was too tired to pretend her heart wasn't bruised. "I guess I'll turn in and get an early start tomorrow. Good night."

"Sara?"

She'd already turned toward the door, and she closed her eyes, tempted to walk out without acknowledging him. "Yes?"

He paused a long time. All she could hear was her heart pounding in her ears. And then he said, "Good night."

"THERE'S the van!" Denise ran from the window to the door and burst outside to greet her mother.

Ethan followed her, prepared to carry in Jenna's things. His timing had been good. He'd only arrived five minutes ago and hadn't even seen Sara yet. He knew he should have been here earlier to help her clean out the room, but he still couldn't face her. Instead, when he'd called earlier to tell the kids about Jenna, he'd asked Erika to help her.

Last night he'd had a hell of a time getting to sleep. And when he finally had, erotic dreams of Sara kept waking him up in a sweat. He'd awoken for the final time with a lousy headache and so aroused he could hardly think.

If it weren't for his sister coming today, he would have stayed as far the hell away as he could.

Jenna climbed out of the van and was nearly tackled by Denise. She laughed as she hugged her daughter, picked her up in the air and swung her around. Just like he used to do with her.

It was weird watching her, all grown up with children of her own. Twelve years ago, he'd have sworn it would be him playing with his own children. The thought brought a knot to his chest.

Erika came out behind him and rushed to join her mom and sister. "I can't believe you made it here for Christmas! And that you got rid of the dork. Way to go, Mom!"

Jenna sighed and tugged at Erika's hair. "He wasn't a dork. He just wasn't right for me. Now give me a hug before I tell Santa to give you a lump of coal."

Erika rolled her eyes, and with gruff affection, circled her arms around her mother.

The scene lightened Ethan's mood. He waited until the girls had had their fill, and then he hugged Jenna, too. "I'm glad you slept through the night. You look better today."

"You don't," she said, frowning at him. "What's up?"

"Christmas shopping wiped me out."

She snorted. "You'd rather herd cattle or mend fences?"

"No contest."

"Come on, you big goof." She linked her arm in his and started toward the house. "Buy me a cup of coffee, will ya?"

He held back. "You go on. I'll get your stuff unloaded."

"There's plenty of time for that. Besides, I want the girls to bring in the small things." She lowered her voice to a whisper. "It's a good way to expend some of that energy that can drive you crazy."

Grudgingly, he let her pull him along.

"Erika, Denise, you guys start bringing the stuff inside. But don't carry anything heavy," she called back to the girls, and when Denise started to whine, she added, "And no peeking in packages or suitcases."

Denise's eyes lit up and she quickly took the box Erika handed her.

Ethan snorted. "Well, you know they're going to look now."

Jenna grinned. "Let them. I haven't bought their presents yet. I just figured they needed a little motivation."

He opened the door and stared at Jenna for a moment, then burst out laughing. "You sly little devil. You haven't changed."

"Yes, I have." She flipped her hair off her shoulder and went inside.

He followed, and came face-to-face with Sara as she rounded the corner. His grin immediately faded. Sara's eyes clouded with hurt.

"Good morning," he said, aware of Jenna's wide-eyed interest. "I got here only a few minutes ago."

Sara nodded, and smiled at Jenna. "Hi," she said, offering her hand. "I'm Sara Conroy."

Jenna was momentarily speechless. "Hi, I'm, well, you know who I am," Jenna broke off, laughing. She looked from Ethan back to Sara. "I didn't expect you at all."

Sara blinked at Ethan. "You said you told her I was watching the girls."

"Oh, he did," Jenna said quickly. "I meant, I didn't realize you were so young and pretty."

Sara blushed and wrung her hands together.

Ethan wanted to give his sister a good swift kick in her behind. "I thought you wanted coffee."

"I do. We can all have some while you two tell me how this came about." She waved a hand between Ethan and Sara.

He passed a weary hand over his face and blew into his palm. "Sara posted an ad. I called. She accepted the position. End of story."

"I really don't have time for coffee right now," Sara said, backing away. "Maybe later."

Jenna didn't say anything, but her gaze was bright with curiosity as it landed on Ethan, and a knowing smile began to lift the corners of her mouth.

As glad as he was to see her, Ethan still wanted to give his sister a swift kick in the behind.

IT HAD been easy for Sara to avoid Jenna yesterday. It was her first day home and her daughters were excited and demanded most of her time. Even Misty opened up around her and readily called her Aunt J. Not surprising. Jenna was funny and outgoing and energetic. She was pretty, too, though with her blond hair and light hazel eyes, she looked nothing like Ethan. Good thing. Sara would hate the constant reminder of him. She felt crummy enough already.

He hadn't been around much, and when he had, he spent time with his sister and the girls. Sara hadn't expected anything else, but seeing him and thinking about him still hurt.

She had just put on a second pot of coffee when Jenna entered the kitchen with Denise, who as usual, was trying to finagle something out of her mother. Sara smiled to herself. She liked what she knew of Jenna, but what she truly admired was her kindness and patience with the kids.

"Denise, knock it off." Jenna tugged at her daughter's ponytail. "Or I'm gonna have a talk with Santa."

Denise sighed dramatically, and then she looked at Sara and her eyes suddenly widened. "Hey, what happened to all the presents you and Uncle Ethan bought the other day? You said you would wrap them and put them under the tree."

"Oh, you don't need them before—" Sara's teasing words died when she saw the startled look on Jenna's face. A few seconds later, Sara got it. Jenna had just realized that Sara had been with Ethan the other night.

Oh, great.

"Deni." Jenna gave her daughter's ponytail another playful tug. "Why don't you go play with

Misty while I make lunch? After you eat I promise we'll go shopping.''

Oh, even better, Sara thought sarcastically as Denise scampered off. Sara quickly dried her hands. ''Good, if you're making lunch, I'll go wrap those presents.''

''Not so fast.''

Sara narrowed her gaze at the other woman. ''Excuse me?''

Jenna grinned and pulled out two chairs. ''That look may work on the kids, but if you think you'll make it out of here without telling me what's going on, I've got news for you.''

Sara pursed her lips. It was hard not to like this woman, even when she was being pushy. ''Nothing is going on.''

''Right.'' Then Jenna made a funny face. ''I interrupted the other night, didn't I?''

Sara laughed and groaned at the same time. She was too tired to do anything else. ''I'm not having this conversation with you.''

''You're right,'' Jenna said, and Sara sagged with relief. ''I'll have it with Ethan.''

Sara glared at the sly look Jenna gave her. And then she took the chair Jenna had pulled out. ''Now I know who Denise gets her ornery streak from.''

Jenna's smile turned wry. ''Don't get me wrong. I'm not trying to be nosy. I love my brother, and I want the best for him. But talk about stubborn…'' Her expression sobered. ''You know about Emily.''

Sara cast a guilty glance at the back door. Ethan could come in at any moment. ''I know she's his late wife.''

"That's it?"

Sara nodded, afraid to ask for information, afraid Jenna wouldn't volunteer.

Jenna stared in thoughtful silence before she asked, "Did he tell you about our parents' death and him raising me?" Sara nodded, and Jenna continued, "Ethan has always had too much responsibility dumped on him, and he takes it so seriously."

"And that's a bad thing?"

"Sometimes. When you neglect to live your own life. Ethan's pretty much stopped with our parents' death. I gave him a really hard time that I'm not proud of, and then there was Emily." A sad smile curved Jenna's lips. "She was always so sweet that when I was younger I thought she was a phony. But that was Emily. She and Ethan dated from the time they were fifteen."

Sara shifted and glanced at the door again. As curious as she was, it made her uneasy to discuss Ethan. "Jenna, why are you telling me all this?"

"Because I know my brother, and this is the first sign of life I've seen in him in a long time. I think you have something to do with it."

"But you haven't been around." Sara bit her lip. She hadn't meant to sound unkind. Fortunately, Jenna didn't seem offended.

"We still talk on the phone and exchange letters. Believe me, I know how much he's isolated himself. That's why I telegraphed him about the girls. So he couldn't say no. Of course I had my own selfish reasons for wanting him to take them, but I wanted to force him out of his cave, too."

Sara liked Jenna even more now.

"Besides, the girls share my opinion about you two, and you know how perceptive kids can be."

Sara gaped at her. "What did they say?"

"Nothing, really. I just picked up on some things."

"This is horrible."

"I promise it's nothing. I shouldn't have brought it up. The girls and I are close, and we've been gabbing a lot. Especially since I've been feeling guilty." She sank back and briefly stared at the ceiling. "Ethan probably told you I was getting married. Stupid me. I thought a man could fix everything. But that's another story.

"Anyway, as much as I liked Emily, I always thought it was a shame how they ended up married so young. Believe me, I know." Jenna sighed. "Emily's mother had left when she was a child, so when Em's father passed away, Ethan married her. She was already twenty and capable of taking care of herself, but that's Ethan, feeling responsible for everyone."

"Oh, no." Sara shook her head. "He married her because he loved her. You don't grieve for someone that long unless—"

"I know he did. That's not what I'm saying. It's just that Ethan hasn't allowed himself many choices." Jenna exhaled. "It's hard to explain. He rides to the rescue before he thinks, and then if it doesn't work out—" She stared off, falling into another meditative silence. Then her gaze met Sara's. "Did he tell you how Emily died?"

The outer door creaked open, drawing both women's attention. They could see Ethan in the mudroom stomping the snow and slush off his boots, and once again silence fell.

"Hey, knucklehead," Jenna greeted him. "Don't you know better than to go out on a day like this?"

He grunted something, slid a glance at Sara.

Sara immediately stood. "I forgot I had some wash to dry. I'll make some lunch in a while."

Ethan watched her hurry out of the kitchen, and his heart sank. She was still skittish around him. He wished he knew what to say to her. He'd still been angry yesterday, and had basically ignored her. What a jerk he was.

"What's with the long face?" Jenna asked, her amused gaze meaningfully swinging toward the door through which Sara had just disappeared. "Let me guess—"

"Not now, Jenna."

Her expression sobered immediately, and she got up and gave him a hug. He'd had more physical contact in the past two weeks than he had had in six years. At times it still felt awkward, but he gave her a one-armed hug back.

She smiled up at him. "What went wrong?"

He gave her a blank look.

"Don't give me that. You know I'm talking about Sara."

He shook away from Jenna. "Nothing I want to discuss."

"Everything had to be going well the night you two were at the motel. Is the problem because of me?"

He shot her a stunned look.

"Sara didn't say anything. Denise said Sara went shopping with you and I put two and two together."

"Great, suddenly you're good at math." He sank into the chair Sara had left.

She chuckled, and stood behind him to massage his neck. "Come on, tough guy. Tell me what happened. You both look miserable."

Ethan warily looked over his shoulder at her. "She does?"

"Well, no kidding."

He snorted. "I don't know why…she's the one who—" Then he winced. This was his kid sister he was talking to.

"Who did what?" Jenna's knowing smile annoyed him. When he stayed stubbornly silent, she said, "Shall we say—threw a wet blanket on things?"

He gave a grudging shrug. "Yeah, you could say that."

"Hmm." She stopped the massage and sat across from him, a puzzled frown on her face. "Did you argue about something?"

"I think I'd remember that."

She ignored his sarcasm. "Did the problem start before or after you saw me?"

"After." He was insane for having this conversation with her. No good would come of it.

Jenna frowned again. "I could talk to her."

"No, you won't." He stood.

"Wait a minute. Did she know who I was?"

"Of course she knows who you are."

"No, I mean, when we accidentally met in the parking lot. She wouldn't have known who I was then.'' Jenna made a waving gesture with her hand he remembered well. "What if she was watching us, and thought maybe…"

He shook his head. "No, she couldn't see us from the room."

"Are you sure?"

"It doesn't matter. I told her who you were." He thought back a moment. "Right away, I think."

"So? What did she do? Me, I would've been good and steamed by then, clobbered you first and asked questions later."

Ethan sat back down and tried to concentrate. "But after I explained, there'd be no reason for her to be upset."

"Maybe she was embarrassed or—" She shrugged. "I don't know Sara. You do. What do you think?"

Totally bewildered, Ethan stared at the empty doorway. For cripes' sake. Could Jenna be right?

Chapter Sixteen

"Sara, can I talk to you?"

"Ouch!" She hadn't heard Ethan approach, and in her surprise, she nicked herself with the knife she was washing.

"What happened?" He was beside her in a second, grasping the finger she tried to examine. "Did you cut yourself?"

"It's just a scratch." She tugged her hand away and applied pressure to the small cut. "What did you want?"

"Let me help finish these dishes, and then let's go someplace where we can talk."

"About what?"

He glanced nervously over his shoulder.

"Jenna is making sure the girls get washed up," she said. "We can talk now if you want." She plunged her hands into the soapy water so he wouldn't see how much they were shaking.

"No. We have to talk in private."

Her heart thudded. "Want to give me a hint what it's about?"

He laid a tentative hand on her arm. "About us. About how foolish I've been. How sorry I am."

She'd already started to melt when he touched her, but the sincere timbre of his voice, the earnestness in his eyes did her in. "I've been foolish, too. I saw you with Jenna the other night, and I'm embarrassed to admit it, but I thought that..." She swallowed around the lump hardening in her throat.

"Of course you did." He slid his arms around her, pulling her back against his chest and resting his chin atop her head. "I would have thought the same thing if the situation were reversed. Except I would've torn someone's head off. I can't believe I didn't figure it out."

"What about me? I kept my mouth shut like a big pansy."

"Hmm, you smell good for a pansy."

She laughed and turned around in his arms. Glancing at the doorway first, she then tiptoed up and kissed him. It was brief, but she still couldn't believe she had the nerve to do it. An hour ago she'd been wondering if she and Misty would be here for Christmas in three days. With Jenna here, Ethan didn't need Sara.

"Tease me like that and I just may have to take you out to the barn for a good scolding."

Excitement spiraled from her toes to her over-imaginative brain. "Do tell."

He smiled and lowered his head.

"But, Ethan, the girls..."

"...are with Jenna."

His lips were soft and warm at first, and then his hunger took over, and his tongue demanded entry.

She gladly received him, and in their sensual fog it took a few moments to realize someone had knocked on the door.

She tried to break away. "Someone's at the door." The words came out garbled when he wouldn't retreat.

"Probably Sam," he murmured, running a hand along the curve of her buttocks.

It wasn't easy but she pushed away from him. "Somebody has to get it. Better it's us."

He exhaled sharply, then gave her a groggy, lop-sided smile. "Right."

They went to the front door together, Ethan slightly ahead of her, and when he opened it Sara stared in shocked disbelief. The floor seemed to sway under her, and she grabbed the nearest thing she could for support. It happened to be Ethan's arm.

Her mouth went totally dry, and her first attempt to speak failed. She tried again. "Cal! What are you doing here?"

Her ex-husband's steely blue gaze fell on the hand she'd clamped around Ethan's arm before it rose with mocking intensity to bore into hers. "Hello, Sara."

The muscles on Ethan's forearms had tightened and she glanced up to see his jaw flex. She let go and subtly edged her way in front of him. "What do you want, Cal?"

"May we come in?" His thin lips curved in the smile that used to make Sara's heart flutter. Now she felt nothing. Not even anger, which was the true blessing. "It's darn chilly out here."

It finally sunk in that he'd said "we." Sara tilted her head to the side, and at the same time, a tall blond woman, younger than Sara, stepped out from behind Cal.

"This is Tiffany," Cal said, and slid a possessive arm around her waist.

She lifted her hand in a feeble wave. "Hi."

Sara mentally shook her head. She didn't know the woman, but she felt sorry for her already. Cal liked them young so he could mold and manipulate.

"Come in," Sara finally said, after getting a nod from Ethan. "But don't plan on staying long."

Cal responded with an amused look as he crossed the threshold into the foyer and shrugged out of his cashmere coat. Tiffany seemed uncomfortable. Ethan just stared at Sara, and then at Cal.

Erika rounded the corner. "Who was at—?" She stopped when she saw Cal and Tiffany. "Hi."

Sara wanted to scream. Instead, she made the introductions, then asked, "Ethan and Erika, would you mind making some coffee?"

"I'd be glad to help," Tiffany quickly offered.

"Oh, that's all right. You don't mind, do you?" Sara gave Ethan a pleading look. She'd seen the anger flash in his eyes as soon as she mentioned Cal's name. She didn't want trouble. Just to get rid of Cal. As for Tiffany, Sara figured she'd at least give the woman the opportunity to hear what kind of jerk Cal was.

"Sure." Ethan gave Cal a warning look before herding Erika toward the kitchen.

"How did you find me?" Sara asked after they'd

disappeared and she'd motioned for Cal and Tiffany to sit in the living room.

"You used your credit card in Andersonville. It was easy for the detective I hired to locate you after that." He looked so smug some of the old anger slithered up Sara's spine.

"You didn't have to hire a detective. I told you I'd call."

"After kidnapping our daughter?"

Sara's blood pressure soared. "Oh, by the way, Misty is fine. She's having her bath." Cal blinked. Tiffany slid him a sharp look. "About the kidnapping, that's a lie and you know it. You very clearly told me to go ahead and leave, that I couldn't make it on my own." Sara shrugged. "Shouldn't say things you don't mean, Cal."

His eyes lit with surprise, and she knew what he was thinking—that she'd changed, that she was bolder now, more self-assured. Good thing she'd slid her hands under her thighs so he couldn't see how badly they shook.

"Don't worry, Sara, I'm not pressing charges." He had snake-like eyes, and his chin was too pointed. Funny, she hadn't noticed before now. "Unless, of course, you're unreasonable."

"You have no grounds to press charges," she said with a flippancy she wished she felt. "And we both know I've always been reasonable. Too reasonable."

"Then you'll understand why I'm taking Misty back to Dallas with me."

Sara stared dumbfounded at him. "You're insane."

Ethan had carried a tray into the living room in time to hear Cal's vile declaration. Sara was an inch away from clawing the weasel's eyes out. Ethan wouldn't care. He'd understand, her flustered mind told her.

Good thing only a bowl of sugar, a small pitcher of cream and some spoons were on the tray. Ethan set it down with so much force, the coffee table shook.

"You came a long way for nothing, Conroy." Ethan's eyes blazed with anger as he straightened and glared at Cal. Of course Sara had already seen him angry, but not like this.

"Ethan, please?" She reached for his hand.

From the hallway, she could hear the girls hounding Jenna about something. In another second Denise led them into the living room. Their chattering stopped immediately when they spotted Cal and Tiffany.

Misty stepped forward, her eyes wide. "Daddy?"

"Sugar plum." Cal grinned and held his arms open.

Misty's gaze flickered to Sara before she moved into his embrace. She hugged his neck and made the usual face when her cheek made contact with his slicked-back hair. "I didn't know you were coming, Daddy."

"Aren't you glad to see me?" He held onto her hands when she stepped back and nodded. "Say hello to my friend Tiffany."

Misty's gaze went first to the blonde's enormous breasts molded by a thin pink sweater. Then smiling shyly, she took the hand Tiffany offered.

"You're even prettier than your dad described." Tiffany gave the girl a genuine smile.

"Honey, would you mind staying with Denise and Aunt Jenna in the back while Daddy and I talk?" Sara shot Jenna a questioning look. She returned a small nod.

"Come on, munchkins, let's go." Jenna grabbed Denise's sleeve when the girl started toward the kitchen. Misty promptly turned to join them.

"Wait a minute." Belligerence tainted Cal's voice. "I think Misty should stay. After all, this concerns her."

Before Sara could protest, Tiffany elbowed him and gave him an appalled look.

"Go ahead, Misty," Sara said quickly, and held her breath until Jenna took them safely away. Astonishingly, Cal said nothing more, but Sara wasn't fooled. He wasn't through yet.

Her gaze briefly swept Ethan. He still looked as angry as all get-out, but, admirably, he was keeping his cool. She still wished he'd go back to the kitchen, though.

She looked at Cal. "What is this about? You never cared whether she was around or not before."

He didn't have the good grace to so much as flinch. Tiffany did, though. "It's the holidays, and I want to spend time with my daughter. What's so unusual about that?"

Sara gave him a you've-got-to-be-kidding look. "It's your parents, isn't it? With Misty missing, the perfect family portrait won't be complete. When are you going to grow up and get out from under their thumbs?"

Bright spots of fury stained his cheeks, and Sara's insides trembled with the knowledge she'd gone too far.

"Don't push me, Sara." His voice was low, deadly. "If this becomes a legal battle, you won't have the resources to win."

"Yes, she will," Ethan said quietly.

"Ethan?" Sara rose and curled an arm around the front of his waist. "Erika probably needs your help."

"I know who you are," Cal said, his narrowed gaze directed at Ethan. "The Double S provides beef for most of the southwest market, so obviously you aren't without financial resources."

Sara stared at Ethan in shock. He didn't deny it. Even though she'd seen the parade of hands come and go, she'd had no idea...

"However," Cal continued, "you don't have the connections I have. So if I were you, I'd keep my nose out of this."

Sara cut Ethan off before he could respond. She stood in front of him and stared directly up into his face until he finally dragged his furious gaze away from Cal and met her eyes.

"Ethan, this is my fight, not yours."

"But, Sara—"

She forced him to back up, toward the dining room, until they were far enough away they couldn't be overheard. "I appreciate your concern and support but I have to do this."

He grabbed her upper arms and squeezed gently. "I want to help. If it comes to it, he's wrong about me not having connections. I know a lot of people, politicians, judges. You don't have to face this alone.''

"Thank you.'' She touched his face. "But I have to handle this by myself. I *need* to handle this. Do you understand?''

He slowly shook his head.

"Then will you just trust me?''

His troubled gaze roamed her face. "Yes.''

She smiled and squeezed his hand. "Give me about five minutes, and then bring in the coffee. I'll signal if I want you to pour it over his fat head.''

Ethan's lips didn't so much as twitch. His gaze lifted over her head in the direction of the living room. She didn't have to guess who was at the receiving end of his deadly glare.

"Five minutes,'' he said before he headed toward the kitchen.

Sara took a deep calming breath before she turned to face Cal. She was still nervous, but if she wanted her bluff to pack the necessary punch, she'd have to be confident and unyielding. He had to believe she'd completely changed from the insecure doormat she once was. He'd already had a taste of it in the past few months, but at times she'd also backed down. That she'd had the gumption to leave had probably panicked him.

"Okay, Cal, this is the way it is,'' she said as she walked briskly toward him, stopping just short of his chair. "I have custody of Misty, which, I'll remind you, you did not oppose in court.'' She paused at his cocky grin, the one that used to send apprehension up her spine. Now it infuriated her. "You're her father and she loves you. Of course I will not block any visitation. But Misty stays with me.''

''Really?'' He lounged back in the chair as if this were his kingdom and Sara a mere subject. ''And if I say otherwise?''

She lifted her chin. ''I already told you what I'm prepared to do. I doubt your father would appreciate that kind of publicity for the Conroy name.''

Cal's oily smile returned. ''You know, I thought about that, Sara, and I finally realized you wouldn't do any such thing.''

Sara raised her brows. ''Wouldn't I?''

He slowly shook his head, his eyes maddeningly confident. ''You'd be too concerned how that would affect Misty.''

Sara's insides crumbled, but she tried to keep her head up. He was right but she couldn't back down. She scrambled for something to say.

''Tell you what,'' Cal said. ''Let's call Misty out here and ask her where she'd rather spend Christmas. Here…'' He glanced around the large but modestly furnished living room. ''Or at my parents' mansion.''

''Leave her out of this,'' Sara said in a low, fierce voice.

''What's the matter, Sara? Afraid you can't compete with the mountain of presents waiting for her? The decorated trees in every room? The traditional visit from Santa on Christmas Eve?''

''I'm warning you, Cal….''

''Maybe we should ask her who she'd rather live with permanently.'' He rose from the chair and made a move toward the hall, and every muscle in Sara's body tightened as she jumped in front of him.

"Cal, sit down." Tiffany was the one who got his attention. He looked at her in astonishment. "Sit."

He didn't comply, nor did he make another move toward the hall. He looked too dumbfounded, his mouth open as he stared at his companion.

Tiffany put one hand on her hip. "What on earth is the matter with you, dragging a child into your personal beef with Sara? You should be ashamed of yourself. You can't ask her to choose between you."

Cal's lips thinned, and color rose in his thin face. "When I want your opinion, I'll ask for it."

"Ha." Tiffany made a sound of disbelief. "That'll be the day." She shook her head. "Misty is a child. She doesn't have the same frame of reference as an adult so she processes things differently. Her view is myopic at this point. Asking her to choose between you and her mother is like asking her to choose which parent she loves more."

Cal blinked and looked at Sara. She almost started laughing when she realized he was looking for help. But all Sara could think was—*You go, Tiffany!*

"That would be cruel," Tiffany's voice lowered persuasively, and she tucked an arm around Cal's. "And I know you don't want to be cruel, do you, honey?"

"Of course not," he muttered irritably. "Tiffany's a graduate student in psychology," he said, glancing at Sara and shaking his head.

She gave him a sympathetic smile. Inside, her heart was doing cartwheels. "She's right," Sara said softly. "We created such a beautiful, intelligent, sensitive child, and she loves both of us. Let's not screw things up now.''

The stubborn glint she knew well gleamed from his eyes as he stared unblinkingly at her.

''Sara's a good mom.'' Tiffany leaned closer and playfully bit his ear. ''You haven't even grown up yet. Misty belongs with her.''

Cal closed his eyes and sighed. Miraculously, when he opened them, the anger and resentment had faded.

Ethan and Erika walked in with the coffee, Ethan looking calm and relatively cool. Sara didn't kid herself. He'd probably been listening. She would've done the same.

Cal glanced at his watch. ''It's late. I think we'd better skip the coffee.''

Sara's heart took flight. This was Cal's way of backing off. He would never come out and say he was wrong, but this was good enough for her. More than good enough. And she wanted to kiss Tiffany.

''I'd like to spend a few minutes with Misty first,'' he said, and Sara's stomach coiled in fear. ''Don't worry, Sara, I just want to reassure her I love her. Even if we can't spend Christmas together.''

His unexpected sincerity touched Sara. ''Of course.''

''Perhaps we can make arrangements for her to come to Dallas for Easter?''

The thought made Sara uneasy. ''One step at a time, okay?''

He didn't look happy with that answer but only shrugged. ''I understand.''

"I'll go get Misty."

"I have something out in the car for her." Cal's demeanor was reserved, thoughtful, and Sara didn't know if she should be suspicious or grateful. "I'll be right back."

When he returned, Misty and Tiffany were waiting for him near the Christmas tree in the den. Jenna kept Denise occupied in her room where Erika joined them. Sara sat with Ethan in the dining room, not so close that they intruded, but Sara could still keep an eye on them, if only for her own peace of mind. Cal was being amazingly attentive to his daughter, which both pleased and worried Sara at the same time.

"I'm proud of you," Ethan said, covering her hand with his, and luring her attention. "You stood up to him."

She smiled wryly. "Yeah, but Tiffany gets first prize, bless her little heart. I have to admit, she surprised me."

He chuckled. "Me, too."

"Hey, how do you know what was going on? You weren't eavesdropping, were you?"

He answered with a lopsided smile.

She smiled back. "I'm proud of you, too. You respected my wishes and didn't rush to my rescue."

"It wasn't easy," he grumbled.

"That's why I'm so proud of you."

His eyebrows furrowed slightly, and his gaze searched her face. Before he could say anything, they heard a large yawn coming from Misty.

Sara glanced at her watch. Way past the kiddo's bedtime. "Guess it's time to break up the party," she said, surprised again by Cal who ruffled Misty's hair with awkward tenderness.

"It's late. Want to let them spend the night?" Ethan motioned with his chin. "He seems to be playing nicely."

With mixed feelings, she watched her ex-husband and daughter. It cheered Sara to see them get along so well, but selfishly, she wanted to get rid of Cal as soon as possible.

Feeling the weight of Ethan's stare, she looked over to find him watching her. It was obvious he'd been furious with Cal only an hour ago, yet how quickly he was willing to forgive and forget. At least to the degree he could be civil and hospitable.

"Sure," she said. "Why not? But you offer."

His eyebrows arched, and he hesitated, before nodding and getting to his feet.

Sitting in a chair near the fireplace, Cal was leaning forward, watching Misty at his feet, playing with the two dolls she'd unwrapped. He looked up warily as Ethan approached, Sara following close behind.

Ethan extended his hand. "Glad you and Sara worked things out. You're welcome to stay the night if you like."

Cal narrowed his gaze and reluctantly shook Ethan's hand. "We need to get home by Christmas Eve. I don't think—"

"We'd love to," Tiffany broke in, looking pointedly at Cal. "That way you can spend a little more time with Misty, and we can still leave first thing in the morning."

Sara hid a smile. *Go Tiffany.*

"Stay, Daddy," Misty said, smiling up at him.

"Since I already opened a present, we can pretend it's Christmas and you can tuck me in."

Cal gazed down at her. This was unfamiliar territory for him, and his uncertainty showed. A pang of sympathy lodged itself in Sara's chest. By distancing himself, he'd already missed so much of his daughter's life.

"Guess it's settled then," he said finally, returning Misty's smile.

Impulsively, Sara said, "Daddy's sorry he can't stay for Christmas, but maybe you can spend Easter with him."

Misty didn't look so sure she wanted to make the commitment, but Cal seemed pleased with the peace offering. It was a start.

"Heck," Ethan said, slipping an arm around Sara's shoulders. "Maybe next year you can come back and spend Christmas here."

That startled everyone. Even Misty, whose eyes grew big and excited. Did Ethan realize what he was saying? Sara stared incredulously at him. His eyes met hers, and she could almost see reality sink in as he visibly swallowed. At any moment, she knew, he'd drop his arm, put an invisible barrier between them.

Instead, he squeezed tighter.

Chapter Seventeen

Ethan waited until he was sure Cal and Tiffany had left before he returned to the house late the next morning. He'd spent a couple of hours swinging an ax, splitting enough firewood for a month, trying to work off the tension tightening his chest and shoulders.

Last night he'd practically asked Sara to stay. Hell, he'd implied he expected her to stay, and that was what he wanted. He hated the thought of how quiet it would be without her and Misty. How dull the sun would seem without Sara's smile. Yet that little voice still reminded him that this was Emily's house.

He trudged up the walkway to the front door, a high-pitched squeal reaching him through the double doors. That had to be Denise. The girl had an amazing pair of lungs. Smiling, he knocked, and was promptly greeted by Jenna.

"It wasn't locked," she said, holding the door open for him. "And if it were, I don't know why you wouldn't just use your key. It is your house, you knucklehead."

He grinned good-naturedly at her childhood name for him, but as he glanced around at the subtle changes Sara had made, it didn't feel like the house he and Emily had shared at all. The art deco style candleholders sitting on the mantle were definitely not Emily's taste. Nor were the aromatherapy candles scattered about. The place looked nice, though, Ethan admitted, just different. It saddened him a little.

"Where's Sara?" he asked.

"She's in the kitchen cleaning up, but don't think you're going to go plant yourself with a cup of coffee." Jenna crooked her finger at him. "We need your brute strength."

"Can't I have one cup first?" he asked, plodding after her down the hallway to the bedrooms.

"This will only take a minute. I need help flipping a mattress." She stopped at the master bedroom door.

"Not in there?"

"Yeah, why?"

"You know what room this is," he said quietly.

Jenna turned away from the door, a sad, sympathetic look on her face and grabbed both his hands. "It's time, Ethan."

"Don't push, Jenna."

"Ethan…"

He pulled out of her grasp. "No one is to go into that room."

Jenna reached out to him again, but a noise coming from inside the bedroom stopped her, and she frowned at the door and then looked quizzically at him.

Another noise. And then giggling.

Ethan's chest constricted, and he threw open the door. Across the bed lay several of the long dresses Emily had favored. A strand of pearls dangled from the bed post. Her favorite cameo earrings had been dropped on the hardwood floor.

Erika stepped into view, her eyes wide and guilty, the neckline of one of Emily's ruffled blouses sliding off her shoulder. She winced and shrunk back. "Uncle Ethan, I didn't know you were here."

"Hi, Uncle Ethan!" Denise blithely stepped out of the closet, trying to balance herself in a pair of Emily's shoes, her white lace wedding veil pinned crookedly to Denise's hair. "Look at me. I'm a princess."

The floor seemed to crumble beneath Ethan's feet. The room swam, spiraling into a whirlpool. "Get out," he said, his voice barely controlled.

"I'm sorry, Uncle Ethan." Erika swiftly pulled off the blouse, nearly taking off her own T-shirt along with it. "We were just playing."

"What's all the commotion?" Sara walked down the hall, smiling, but when she saw that the master bedroom was open, she stopped, a nervous frown etching lines around her mouth.

He ignored Jenna giving Sara a shake of her head, and focused on Erika and Denise. "Out. Now."

"Girls, come on." Jenna moved to help Denise take off the veil.

When Erika stooped to pick up the cameo earrings, Ethan told her to leave them. Without another word, she scooted out of the room. Denise scampered out behind her.

Jenna paused at the doorway. "Ethan?"

He closed his eyes and shook his head. He didn't open them again until he heard her continue down the hall. Only Sara hadn't left. She stood quietly to the side, but said nothing, just stared at him with a haunted look on her face, fear darkening her eyes.

There wasn't a damn thing he could say to reassure her. He wasn't even sure he could speak. Instead he entered the room he hadn't stepped foot in for six years, and closed the door behind him. Emily deserved to have her things restored to order. He prayed he could remember where everything belonged.

SARA TRIED to keep herself busy in the den, dusting and vacuuming, anything to keep her mind off Ethan. Nothing worked. The expression of despair and grief on his face was as vivid to her now as it had been forty minutes ago when she'd hopelessly watched him disappear into the room.

On some level, she understood his desperation to preserve Emily's memory, but as the woman who loved him, Sara's heart was disintegrating more each minute he kept himself isolated in that room, Emily's shrine.

Sara wasn't sure when she had graduated from a mixture of lust and like to love, although she suspected it had grown steadily each time he had treated the girls and herself with a kindness that she knew sometimes cost him, forcing him to relive his grief. Last night, when he'd stepped aside and allowed her to deal with Cal, she'd known she was a goner for sure.

She turned off the vacuum, and thought she heard a door close down the hall. Jenna and the girls had hightailed it to the kitchen, so she knew it wasn't them. She quickly picked up a dust rag and tried to look busy while keeping an eye out for Ethan.

He emerged a moment later, looking no better than he had earlier. Exhaustion tinged his complexion gray, and sadness stole the gleam from his eyes. She didn't know if it would be better to talk to him or to let him be. Her impulse was to try and draw him out, get him to talk about his frustration and anger and pain. But Erika suddenly appeared and voided the decision.

"Uncle Ethan?"

He obviously didn't want to stop and talk, but to his credit, he waited to hear his niece out.

"I'm sorry I went into your room. I—I—" She shrugged sheepishly. "It was my fault. Don't blame Denise and take away the presents on her Santa's list." Her gaze slid briefly to Sara. "Misty wasn't even there so don't blame her either. Staying here on the ranch is still at the top of her list, and she wants it bad."

Ethan's frown showed his confusion, but all he said was, "It's over and done with. I trust you'll know better the next time."

Erika eagerly nodded. "Am I going to be punished?"

He shook his head, looking almost too weary to speak. "Like I said, it's over."

When he strode past Erika toward the front door, Sara hurried after him. "Ethan, wait."

At first she thought he was going to ignore her,

and then he hesitated with his hand on the doorknob. "Can it wait, Sara?" he asked quietly, without looking at her.

She'd have preferred he snapped at her. He sounded so lost it tore at her heart. "I just wanted to remind you that we're going to finish decorating tonight," she said cheerfully. "Tomorrow is Christmas Eve."

"Right."

He left without another word.

Sara stood at the window, her forehead pressed to the cold glass and stared long after his truck had disappeared down the drive. He wouldn't come back tonight, she was certain of that. And she wasn't so sure he'd show up tomorrow.

Already she missed him. Not his physical presence so much as the Ethan she'd glimpsed this past week. The one who could smile and even laugh some. The one who kidded with his nieces and flattered Madge. The Ethan who'd kissed Sara until hope and joy filled her heart.

Sadly, the man who left minutes ago was the same solemn man who'd answered her ad. And who still mourned his dead wife.

IT WASN'T the same. Of course, the shack still looked like it always had, with its wood plank floor, the shabby brown curtain that separated the bedroom from the living area, the old stove that worked only half the time. But it was too quiet. No feminine smells laced the air and seduced Ethan or soothed his wounded soul.

Sara wasn't here.

Ethan lay back on his cot and closed his eyes, hoping the grueling physical work he'd put himself through for the past three hours would induce sleep. He had no business thinking about Sara. He should be thinking about Emily. But she seemed so far away these days. It wasn't fair. Emily had been a good wife, his best friend, and she deserved better than a few flowers placed on her cold grave from time to time.

He turned over onto his stomach, disgusted with himself. This was self-pity talking. He'd honored her memory in every way. He'd never forget her. Ever. The problem was, he couldn't stop thinking about Sara. Which wasn't wrong...except when the sight and smell of her edged Emily out. Made the memories of their life together seem fuzzy.

Just lying here he could almost smell Sara's scent, hear the uplifting tinkle of her laughter. She'd been through hard times, had made tough decisions that affected Misty as well as herself, and Sara had remained strong. He respected and admired her more than he could describe.

He hadn't left a light on, and inside the shack was nearly black but for a few gray shadows. He didn't know what time it was and didn't care. For six years this place had been his home, his sanctuary. Now, he could barely stand to look at the dingy walls and the pine table without a yellow napkin folded into a pretty shape by Sara. He turned his face into the pillow and prayed for sleep.

ETHAN VAGUELY heard the pounding of hooves, rolled over onto his back and squinted as a stream of light flowed across his face. Morning? Already? He struggled to a sitting position, and glanced through bleary eyes at the shabby gray walls. When he heard the whinny of a horse outside, he snapped awake.

Who would ride all the way out to the shack?

Sara?

He reached for his jeans and fumbled into them. By the time he got to the window, someone was knocking at the door.

He swung it open, disappointment needling him. "Hey, Sam. What are you doing out here?"

"Got some news I figured you'd want." Sam's breath filtered through the frosty air, and Ethan motioned him to come in out of the cold, the acceleration of his heartbeat having nothing to do with the frigid air whipping in the door.

"Anything wrong?" There had to be, or Sam wouldn't be here.

"Depends on your point of view." Sam rubbed his gloved hands together and made a shivering noise. "Coldest day this winter yet."

"Come on, Sam."

"Sara's leaving."

Ethan's gut clenched. "Today?"

He shrugged. "Seems so."

Ethan turned to stare out the window. He couldn't let her leave, yet what reason could he give her to stay? She needed a job. He could offer her one.

"Ethan?"

He slowly turned back to Sam, suddenly feeling more vulnerable than he ever had in his life.

"It's over."

"What is?"

"Your penance."

Ethan frowned at his friend, not sure he wanted to hear him out.

Sam's gaze bore into him. "For still being alive when Emily died."

Ethan reared his head back and made a sound of disgust, disbelief. "What the devil are you talking about?"

"All this," Sam gestured around the small room, "living like a hermit. It's no good. Emily wouldn't want you to feel guilty for not drowning with her in that flood. It was a freak accident. Nothing you could have done about it. Emily would want you to live, Ethan, not crawl into the grave after her."

Ethan closed his eyes. "You don't know what you're talking about, Sam." When he opened them again, he sent his friend a warning look.

Sam flipped off his Stetson and stared down into the sweat-stained crown. "I've kept my mouth shut long enough." He met Ethan's gaze. "I understand you want to honor Emily's memory, and you have in every way possible except one. Getting on with your life. Just like she would've wanted."

Anger rumbled in Ethan's gut. He resisted the urge to lash out at Sam and end up saying something he'd regret. But the effort took all of his control.

"Well, I've said my piece." Sam adjusted the Stetson back on his head. "In your heart, you know what's right." He made it to the door and paused. "I like Sara. She's a nice lady. And she cares about you."

Ethan managed to hold his tongue until after the

door closed behind Sam. And then he let out a curse he'd never said before. He'd known Sam all his life. Ethan had thought his friend had understood him these past years. But penance? Sam was wrong.

He was. Dammit.

Rubbing the grit from his eyes, he trudged to the stove and got out a can of coffee, and then stared at it, unable to complete the simple task of measuring out the grounds.

Why the blazes was Sara leaving? It didn't make sense. Misty would want to spend Christmas here with the girls. So would Sara, for that matter. Had he upset her that badly? Was it too much to ask to have Emily's things left in peace?

He abandoned the coffee and went in search of a fresh shirt. Tonight was Christmas Eve. She wouldn't want to be on the road alone with Misty. He could talk her into staying. If not him, Jenna and the girls could do it. Except they obviously hadn't been able to so far.

Fear chilled him, and he quickly buttoned the green flannel shirt he'd found, then reached for his tan suede jacket. Maybe he should just let her go. He had nothing to offer her, and Sara deserved a stable home, a loving husband, someone to help her with Misty. He was too busy doing penance, according to Sam.

Thinking of his friend's words struck a sharp chord of unease deep within him. Ethan set his hat on his head, and then pulled on a pair of leather gloves, anxious to speed through the cold air on Jet's back. A good ride always made him feel better, helped put things into perspective.

By the time he'd saddled and mounted Jet, the thought of never seeing Sara again was almost too much to take. But he still didn't know what to do about it. Could he selfishly ask her to stay and offer nothing in return?

He should never have reopened the house, hired Sara, opened himself up again. Life had been all right until two weeks ago. Now the bleakness seemed unbearable.

Before he realized where he was headed, he saw Emily's grave on the next slope. It was easy to spot with the big red bow Sara had tied on the wreath she'd made for Emily. Sara had shyly given it to him two days ago because she knew Emily loved Christmas, too.

At the reminder, a sudden lump threatened to cut off his air supply, and when he got to the grave, he stumbled out of the saddle. Immediately he hit his knees, his chest so tight and aching he clutched at the cold dirt.

"God, Emily, tell me what to do. You always knew the right thing to say." He closed his eyes and waited for her words to flow through his head. They often did when he came here for peace or guidance. Sometimes he could almost hear her speak as plain as the white marble cross that marked her grave. But not today. Silence stung the air, recriminations churned inside his head.

Was she angry with him for allowing some of the memories to slip away? For allowing another woman into her home?

God, what was wrong with him? Emily wasn't like that. She'd be overjoyed that a little five-year-old girl had a place to spend Christmas, that someone as good and decent as Sara was taking care of the house…was making Ethan smile again.

Maybe she was telling him to let go.

Maybe his penance was over.

He sat back on his heels and blinked away the moisture from his eyes. "I'll always love you, Emily," he whispered, and in the back of his mind he heard Sara's contented sigh.

Jet nosed his shoulder, and Ethan turned and stroked the gelding's neck. "You're right, boy, it's time to go." Ethan struggled to his feet and prayed he wasn't too late.

"YOU'RE SUPPOSED to be in Albuquerque visiting your in-laws. Ethan said you go every Christmas." Jenna's voice had risen in accusation, and Sam just shook his head.

"I'm divorced. Ellie and I split up about a year ago."

"That's no excuse," she mumbled.

Sam frowned. She wasn't making sense. Not even for her. "Look, Jenny, I'm sorry if my being here offends you so—"

"Don't call me that. My name is Jenna."

"Actually, it's Jennifer. How about I call you *that?*"

She lifted her chin, and her blond hair streamed down her back. He could barely keep his eyes off her, even though she could make him so mad he could spit nails.

"I am not going to let you get to me," she said. "It's Christmas Eve, and the girls and I are going to spend it here with Ethan and Sara, and then I'm outta here.''

"Typical," he muttered, and turned away.

"What do you mean by that?'' She grabbed his arm, and the simple touch lit a fire in him so hot he had to take a deep calming breath.

She swiftly withdrew her hand, and with enormous satisfaction, he noticed it shook some. Good. The little wildcat wasn't unaffected either.

"I asked you a question,'' she said, stomping her foot and making her breasts jiggle so he had to look away.

"You're always running away. That's how you handle every problem you've ever had. When are you going to grow up?''

Her eyes narrowed to murderous slits, and she glared at him as if she wanted to strangle him with her bare hands. And then she blinked and moved her head to the side to stare past him. "It's about time," she muttered.

Sam turned around. Ethan was headed toward the house on horseback. Sam smiled. There was hope yet. When he turned back to Jenna, his smile faded. "This isn't over," he said as he broke away to meet Ethan and take care of Jet.

"The hell it isn't,'' she called after him, and Sam smiled again as he stood waiting for Ethan.

"Sara still here?'' Ethan asked as he climbed off Jet and tossed Sam the reins.

Sam just nodded and hoped Ethan wouldn't be too steamed over him lying about Sara. "I think she's in one of the bedrooms. The girls are playing in the barn.''

Ethan paused and clapped a hand on Sam's shoulder. Their eyes met. "Thanks, buddy."

Sam grunted. "Get your sorry butt in there."

Ethan's mouth began to curve as he took the porch steps two at a time, vaguely catching a glimpse of Jenna off to the side. She looked ticked off about something, but he ignored her and kept on going until he heard a noise coming from the end of the hall.

Sara was in her room making her bed. She looked up in surprise when he stopped at the doorway and gave him a tentative smile. "We missed you last night."

He scanned the room for signs of packed bags. There were none. "Yeah, sorry, I got tied up."

She plumped a pillow, then clasped her hands together. "Can we count on you to join us tonight?"

"Tonight?"

"It's Christmas Eve, remember?"

Confusion and relief hit him at once. "You're not leaving?"

Her eyes grew dark and she paled. "Is that what you want?"

"No." He entered the room, and took both her hands in his. "God, no. It's just that Sam said—" Ethan blinked. "That dirty son of a gun."

"Sam told you I was leaving?"

Reluctantly, he nodded.

A pleased smile curved Sara's lips. "And you rushed here to stop me?"

He met her eyes and slowly nodded again.

"Why?"

He dropped her hands, flexed his shoulder. "I

didn't want you and Misty to spend Christmas on the road."

"Is that the only reason?" She seemed incredibly calm, almost as if all she was asking was if he wanted coffee.

"Well, no."

She watched him, her hands once again clasped together as she waited patiently for him to continue.

He realized he still had his hat on, and he quickly whipped it off and held it against his chest.

"Is this going to take a while? Shall we sit down?" Mischief gleamed in her eyes, and he felt a flutter in his belly.

"I want you to stay."

"Okay." She gave a small nod, and then plucked the hat from his hands and threw it on the bed. "Why?"

His chest constricted. He cleared his throat. "Because you haven't finished cleaning all the rooms."

She gave a small jerk of surprise, and her smile wavered.

He took her hand and pulled her toward him. "Because we're going to need them when all the little ones start coming."

Confusion leaped into her eyes as she stared up at him. "What little ones?"

He smiled at her, wondering at his luck to have found her. "I love you, Sara."

Pink bloomed in her cheeks, and her lips curved in the most beautiful smile Ethan had ever seen. "I love you, too, Ethan Slade."

"Enough to marry me?" He slipped his arms around her.

"Try and stop me." She laughed when he picked her up off the floor and swung her around.

"Do you think Misty might want a little brother and sister?"

"Oh, I think we can persuade her," Sara said, breathless and grinning. "Ethan?"

At her suddenly somber look his chest squeezed. He brushed a curl off her cheek.

"I can't replace Emily," she said, her gaze searching his face. "I won't even try."

"I don't want you to. I love you, Sara. You're the woman I want." He kissed her until there was no doubt.

Tyler Brides

It happened one weekend...

Quinn and Molly Spencer are delighted to accept three bookings for their newly opened B&B, Breakfast Inn Bed, located in America's favorite hometown, Tyler, Wisconsin.

But Gina Santori is anything but thrilled to discover her best friend has tricked her into sharing a room with the man who broke her heart eight years ago....

And Delia Mayhew can hardly believe that she's gotten herself locked in the Breakfast Inn Bed basement with the sexiest man in America.

Then there's Rebecca Salter. She's turned up at the Inn in her wedding gown. Minus her groom.

Come home to Tyler for three delightful novellas by three of your favorite authors: Kristine Rolofson, Heather MacAllister and Jacqueline Diamond.

HARLEQUIN®
Makes any time special ™

From bestselling
Harlequin American Romance author

CATHY GILLEN THACKER

comes

TEXAS VOWS

A McCABE FAMILY SAGA

Sam McCabe had vowed to always
do right by his five boys—but after
the loss of his wife, he needed the small-town security
of his hometown, Laramie, Texas, to live up to that
commitment. Except, coming home would bring him
back to a woman he'd sworn to stay away from.
It will be one vow that Sam can't keep....

On sale March 2001

Available at your favorite retail outlet.

HARLEQUIN®
Makes any time special ™

#1 *New York Times* bestselling author

NORA ROBERTS

brings you more of the loyal and loving,
tempestuous and tantalizing Stanislaski family.

Coming in February 2001

The Stanislaski Sisters

Natasha and Rachel

Though raised in the Old World traditions of their
family, fiery Natasha Stanislaski and cool, classy
Rachel Stanislaski are ready for a *new* world of love....

And also available in February 2001 from
Silhouette Special Edition, the newest book in the
heartwarming Stanislaski saga

CONSIDERING KATE

Natasha and Spencer Kimball's daughter Kate turns her
back on old dreams and returns to her hometown, where
she finds the *man* of her dreams.

Available at your favorite retail outlet.

Silhouette®

Where love comes alive™

CELEBRATE VALENTINE'S DAY WITH HARLEQUIN®'S LATEST TITLE—

Stolen Memories

Available in trade-size format, this collector's edition contains three full-length novels by *New York Times* bestselling authors Jayne Ann Krentz and Tess Gerritsen, along with national bestselling author Stella Cameron.

TEST OF TIME by **Jayne Ann Krentz**—
He married for the best reason.... She married for the only reason.... Did they stand a chance at making the only reason the real reason to share a lifetime?

THIEF OF HEARTS by **Tess Gerritsen**—
Their distrust of each other was only as strong as their desire. And Jordan began to fear that Diana was more than just a thief of hearts.

MOONTIDE by **Stella Cameron**—
For Andrew, Greer's return is a miracle. It had broken his heart to let her go. Now fate has brought them back together. And he won't lose her again...

Make this Valentine's Day one to remember!

Look for this exciting collector's edition on sale January 2001 at your favorite retail outlet.

HARLEQUIN®
Makes any time special ™

Visit us at www.eHarlequin.com

PHSM

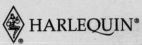
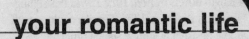

HARLEQUIN®
AMERICAN ◆ ROMANCE®

and **Muriel Jensen**
present

WHO'S THE
DADDY?

*A*t a festive costume ball, three identical
sisters meet three masked bachelors.

*E*ach couple has a taste of true love behind
the anonymity of their costumes—but
only one will become parents
in nine months!

Find out who it will be!

November 2000
FATHER FEVER #858

January 2001
FATHER FORMULA #855

March 2001
FATHER FOUND #866

HARLEQUIN®
Makes any time special ™

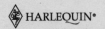
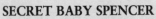